JOE CRAIG

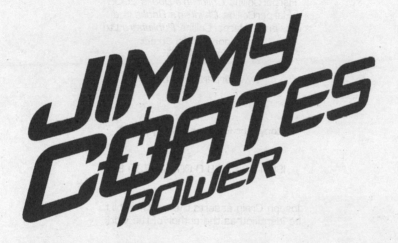

JIMMY COATES POWER

HarperCollins *Children's Books*

First published in Great Britain by
HarperCollins *Children's Books* 2008
HarperCollins *Children's Books* is a
division of HarperCollins *Publishers* Ltd
1 London Bridge Street
London SE1 9GF

www.harpercollins.co.uk

ISBN 13: 978 0 00 727730 8

Joseph Craig asserts the moral right to
be identified as the author of the work.

Printed and bound by CPI Group (UK) Ltd, Croydon, CRO 4YY

MIX
Paper from
responsible sources
FSC® C007454

FSC is a non-profit international organisation established to promote the
responsible management of the world's forests. Products carrying the FSC
label are independently certified to assure consumers that they come
from forests that are managed to meet the social, economic and
ecological needs of present and future generations.

Find out more about HarperCollins and the environment at
www.harpercollins.co.uk/green

Thank you to Sarah Manson, Ann Tobias,
Marc Berlin, Sophie Birshan, Miriam Craig,
Oli Rockberger and everyone at HarperCollins,
particularly Stella Paskins.

Thank you also to:
Catriona Savage, for help with the French
Dr Anna Gorringe, for medical advice
Greg John, for use of his flat,
and Sacha Wilson, legend.

To Mary-Ann Ochota, *always*.

01 THE MESSAGE

"This is Jimmy Coates..."

The boy paused and stared harder into the lens of the tiny camera attached to the top of the computer monitor. His eyes didn't flicker. "I mean, I am Jimmy Coates." He could hear his voice trembling, but he knew he had to go on. He had to get his message out – tell his story. Tell people the truth.

"This is going to sound like the craziest—" He cut himself short, startled by a noise behind him. He looked round. The glow from the lamp-post outside filtered through the slats of the Venetian blinds and the rain on the windows, lighting the small second-floor office in disfigured orange lines, like diseased skin. Nothing had changed.

He glanced again at the infrared detector in the corner of the ceiling. He knew it wouldn't be flashing. Only minutes earlier he'd disabled the office's alarm system. But if anybody passed by the building they might notice the gleam from the computer screen. If they investigated any further and saw Jimmy's makeshift rewiring of the entry system at the door, they'd certainly call the police. There wasn't meant to be anybody in the office of the *Hailsham Gazette* this late at night.

"I know I look like a normal boy," Jimmy went on, trying to steady his breathing so he could get the words out. "I'm twelve. But..." Again he stopped himself. His mouth wouldn't form the words. They raced through his head, but he couldn't force them out. He wanted to scream everything at once: *I'm the perfect assassin. They made me that way. They designed my DNA in a test tube...*

At the same time he knew that some parts of the truth were better left out. Nobody would believe him, and if they did, they'd be terrified instead of listening to what he had to say.

Jimmy forced himself to concentrate and adjusted the direction of the webcam, making sure his face was clear on the monitor. It was so strange seeing himself like this. His features didn't look like his own. His cheeks were thinner and his eyes looked grey.

But in front of him on the desk was something that strengthened his resolve. It was the latest edition of the *Gazette*. The headline leapt out: BRAVE BRITAIN TO HIT BACK AFTER FRENCH ATTACK OUR OIL RIG.

"The Government is lying," continued Jimmy. "The French didn't attack the oil rig. They're just telling everybody that, and like always they're controlling the newspapers and TV and the Internet..." Jimmy half-scrunched the newspaper in frustration. "But now they should know it isn't true. I'm the proof. I blew it up – by accident." His words rushed out in a torrent. "Everybody has to know. If the Government carries on with plans for war, everyone needs to know their reasons for it are a lie. People will die for nothing."

He stopped and took a deep breath. It felt like there was so much more to say, but before he could go on, he saw a reflection in the screen. A blue flash. He'd stayed too long. The police were coming.

"Spread this message," he insisted into the webcam. "And protest every way you can. I know you can't vote, but..." Again he tailed off. The Government had abolished voting when they created Neo-democracy, so Jimmy wondered what possible way there could be to protest about anything. The sound of a siren cut through his thoughts.

"Just spread this message," Jimmy pleaded. "Tell everyone."

He shut off the webcam. It took him less than a minute to post the clip of himself on as many video-sharing websites as he could think of. He knew Government censors would remove it as soon as they found it. They might even shut down the websites completely. He just had to hope that enough people would see it first, and that they'd even spread it themselves on to other sites.

Next Jimmy found the newspaper's publishing software and quickly set up some new headlines for the *Gazette*:

FRENCH DIDN'T ATTACK.
NO REASON FOR WAR WITH
FRANCE. GOVERNMENT LYING.

He knew they would never dare to publish anything like that, but Jimmy thought that if the staff saw them, maybe they could also spread the message.

The wail of sirens was louder now and the whole office was filled with the flashing blue light. Jimmy jumped up from the computer and dashed towards the door, taking the half-scrunched newspaper with him. He could feel his brain counting off the seconds before the police came charging in. Every muscle urged him to race away to safety, but as his hand settled on the door handle one thought held him back: maybe somewhere in this news office would be information about what had happened to his family. Maybe he could even track them down and rebuild his life. A normal life.

Jimmy could sense tiny vibrations in the floor. Somebody else had breached the building. He could feel the muscles in his thighs tightening to force him to run. *Stay*, he pleaded with himself. But Jimmy was fighting his own mind and body. Inside his skin were two beings interwoven. Only one was human.

38 per cent of Jimmy's DNA was identical to that of any other human being in the world. The rest was the template for something entirely new. An organic assassin. Not robot

or machine, but even more deadly. A custom-designed being meant to kill for the British Government. His future had been programmed into his blood. It was his human side that constantly resisted that future. And that's what had turned him from the Government's finest weapon into their number one target.

The assassin instincts in Jimmy were growing stronger by the day. He was designed to be fully operational at the age of eighteen, when his human feelings would be completely controlled by his assassin DNA. But extreme danger had kick-started his development early. He had no idea how long it would be before the assassin in him would take over completely, or what that would feel like. All he knew was that time was running out.

Every second of his life he felt that tension inside him. Now it was as painful as ever. The assassin in him was efficiently marshalling his body as if he were on a mission. Escape. Survival. And rationally, Jimmy knew he should trust that instinct. Yet at the same time he could see the faces of his mother Helen, his sister Georgie and his best friend Felix. Were they still together? Were they still alive? He longed to comb the office, to study every memo, article and report. Somebody must have news of what had happened to them.

BAM!

He'd hesitated too long. The door jolted open. The wood smacked against Jimmy's shoulder and the handle stabbed into his ribs. Before he could react, an enormous figure barrelled into the room. Another followed – two huge policemen, made even more bulky by the Hawk-801 body armour. Jimmy was knocked to the floor, but his powers were already working, fizzing through him.

His fingers had locked around the door handle and as he fell he kicked out, jamming his heel into the lowest hinge. With a crack of splintering wood, the door came free from its frame and followed Jimmy down. Before the two policemen even had time to turn their heads, Jimmy jumped up, leaning his shoulder into the door. It battered the first policeman, then Jimmy kicked the bottom half of it up to crunch one edge into the second man.

Through their grunts and moans, Jimmy picked out two noises. One was the crackle of a police radio. Back-up was on the way. The second noise was the click of a Sig Sauer P229 sidearm.

Jimmy didn't want to wait to find out whether they'd really shoot a child. He couldn't even be sure that they'd seen who it was in the room – that's how fast Jimmy had moved. Instead he charged towards the empty doorway. If back-up was on the way, that meant there was probably nobody covering the corridor or the exterior of the building.

Then came the shot. To Jimmy the sound of it wasn't terrible. It wasn't even shocking. All human responses had shrunk away, swamped in an instant by his programmed instincts. The small explosion of the gun was almost pathetic compared to how Jimmy had anticipated it in his mind. And the anticipation of an assassin had yet again saved his life.

Jimmy had already twisted the unhinged door to hold it behind his back. The bullet imbedded itself in the wood with a feeble thud. Another shot followed, but by then Jimmy had dropped the door and disappeared.

While his limbs pumped with such power and speed, Jimmy felt supremely calm. It was as if his nerves were coated in something that numbed them to the fear, but still heightened his alertness. He raced out of the building, feeling almost as if he was flying. The drizzle on his face felt refreshing. The sirens in his ears were like hunting horns, driving him on faster and harder.

Jimmy knew exactly where he was going. Hailsham was only a small town and his system had easily absorbed the layout of the streets. More than that, he was suddenly aware that his legs were powering him along a predetermined escape route. The assassin had already planned for this.

He pounded away from the high street, cutting through the stillness, a bolt of heat in the rain. His steps reverberated louder as he left the sirens further behind. He wove along the residential streets of endless, identical houses, then cut through an industrial estate and vaulted the iron fence at the back in one huge leap.

Now security lights gave way to darkness, but Jimmy had no doubt where he was. He'd found his way back to the playing field of All Saints School, where he'd arrived earlier that night. Despite the mud, his pace hardly dropped. In seconds he had crossed two football pitches and was climbing into the cockpit of a Tiger Hellfire IV helicopter, which was just where he'd left it.

His chest heaved, but every breath of cold air seemed to pull in more strength to keep him going. Before he'd even strapped on his helmet, his hands were already darting over the controls and the chopper rose several metres off the turf. He carefully balanced the roll of the machine, but at the same time he reached into his pocket and pulled out the crumpled ball of newspaper he'd snatched at the office. There was one thing he had to find: a doctor.

For a second Jimmy was mesmerised by his fingertips. A blue tint had bloomed across his nails and into the skin alongside. It seemed to glow in the faint light, reflecting the LED display on the chopper's control panel. The sight made Jimmy feel sick. So far this was the only visible damage from the one thing that put him in more immediate danger than anything else. More than the police scouring the town for him, more than the British Secret Services, more yet than the assassin instincts inside him that were gradually overwhelming his human mind. As if all that wasn't enough, he had radiation poisoning.

The French Secret Service had tricked him and left his body damaged by massive over-exposure to uranium and actinium. A fully human body would have been destroyed by now, Jimmy was sure. But he had no idea how the radiation was affecting him. He just knew he had to find a doctor who could help him as soon as possible. He scrabbled through the pages of the newspaper. His eyes scanned the text with the processing speed of a computer, letting each sheet fly away into the night when he was finished with it. At last he came to a directory of local health services.

By now he had brought the helicopter above the line of the buildings around the field. He hovered there. Where should he go? He studied the tiny print, his eyes' natural night-vision enhancing the available light.

Jimmy knew it would take luck to find a doctor who would examine him willingly. He was an enemy of the State, and anybody helping him would surely be found and punished. But he knew that out there were other people against the system of Neo-democracy. Jimmy had to find a doctor who not only had the expertise to treat radiation poisoning, but wasn't afraid to stand up to the Government.

A thought burst into life. *If the doctor's afraid*, it hissed, *use force*.

Jimmy's heart jolted at the violence in his own head. The power of the darkness inside him was growing and it shocked him, even though he knew that in this case it was right. He would probably have to at least threaten violence to convince a doctor to help him.

He scrunched up the last sheet of the *Hailsham Gazette* and hurled it out of the cockpit. There was only one place Jimmy had any chance of finding a hospital with the right, modern equipment – and the right doctor. He ran his fingers over the control units of the chopper and tore through the sky towards London. In seconds, he was away from Hailsham, soaring over open country.

Suddenly, Jimmy heard a sound. A distant thud. His eyes jumped to the horizon. At first all he could make out were the shapes of the clouds against the night sky. Then he picked out a tiny flash. Soon there was another just alongside it. They disappeared behind a cloud for a second, then emerged brighter. *Not brighter*, thought Jimmy. *Closer*.

Only then did the helicopter's 2012 four-beam Doppler radar system confirm it. Two planes. It hadn't taken long for the police to identify who had broken into the local newspaper, and these days the Secret Service kept a constant watch on the police. Jimmy's only surprise was that it had taken them this long to send the Royal Air Force.

He felt a sudden swirl of panic that his programming quickly crushed. *Forward*, he heard throbbing in his brain. *Faster*. But the chopper wasn't fast enough. His ears could pick out the sounds of the two planes ripping through the clouds towards him. He was exposed. A single shot would take him out.

With the flick of a finger he shut off the lights on his helicopter. The Nomex Honeycomb panels and Kevlar skin of the chopper made tracking it by radar almost impossible at the best of times. If Jimmy stayed dark and low enough he could escape precision guidance systems on the planes' missiles. Now the pilots would have to rely on their own aim, and that gave Jimmy his chance.

The display on his control panel still glowed, as did the banks of LED lights and switches. Even that was too bright. Jimmy didn't want to give the planes any chance of seeing what they were aiming at. His hands darted across the controls, overriding the onboard computer to shut off any system that gave off a light.

Now Jimmy's senses prickled, heightening his awareness in a way he'd never experienced before. Every tiny ripple of air tingled the hairs on his forearms. His eyes flickered hundreds of times a second, his night-vision illuminating his path in a faint blue haze, giving his reactions precious extra split-seconds to guide the machine.

He could feel the grip of the assassin on his muscles, holding them steady, guiding his limbs. The power of the Tiger Hellfire surged through the mechanism around him. It was as if his body had a direct connection to the 1200 kW turboshaft engines. His slightest thought impacted on his flight path before he even knew what he was doing.

He crossed a motorway, the helicopter low enough

for the runners to whoosh over the car roofs. He dodged between two lorries expertly. Still he could sense the presence of the planes holding a position above him, like hovering eagles waiting to swoop on a vole.

Even in the darkness Jimmy could see the animals in the fields scampering away. He dipped beneath every telegraph wire, leapt over every fence and swung past the front door of every farmhouse. Meanwhile, the engines rumbled, straining to push the chopper beyond its supposed maximum velocity.

The planes kept pace with him. Their two floodlights danced across the fields with Jimmy, sometimes catching him in their glare, but only for tantalising glimpses. Jimmy was making it impossible for them to fire at him, but he still wasn't getting away. It was no good, he thought. Even if he reached London, he would never be able to land.

Then he realised that NJ7 had no intention of this chase ever making it that far. Rising up from the horizon ahead of him were more than a dozen black dots. A cluster of state-of-the-art military helicopters. Each one held steady, just above the land. Then, as one, a dozen sets of floodlights flashed into life. Jimmy squinted in the glare and felt the sweat break out on his forehead. And NJ7 could see every drop.

02 TUNNEL VISION

There was nowhere to hide. Jimmy wanted to throw up his hands, or brace himself for the explosion of the missiles, but his body wouldn't let him. The lights from the enemy choppers had shown the assassin in him a new way out. They lit up a track that crossed directly between them and Jimmy. And approaching slowly from the right, like a worm across a battlefield, was a train.

Instead of turning his helicopter around, or even slowing down, Jimmy charged straight ahead. The helicopters confronting him did the same, moving towards him as a pack. They were hunters, designed and built to complete a mission with total efficiency – and a zero failure rate.

But so was Jimmy. His eyes locked on to the train. His muscles relaxed when he should have been growing more tense. It was as if some chemical had been injected into his system to make his limbs more supple and give him greater control. But it all came from within.

He was nearing the tracks now, winning the race with the choppers ahead of him. The planes overhead fired two rockets, but Jimmy was already into his defensive manoeuvre. He dodged so quickly that he didn't have time to be afraid. The explosion rocked the cabin, but it was the ground behind him going up in flames, not him.

At last he reached the tracks and turned. The detour to avoid the rockets had worked in his favour. It had given the train time to reach him. Jimmy slowed to keep pace with it and once again brought the chopper as low as it would go, gliding past the telegraph poles, wires and signals, sheltering alongside the last carriage of the train.

The fleet of NJ7 helicopters circled over the top, then wheeled round to follow, just behind the train. Jimmy could almost feel himself smiling, against his will. Something inside him was revelling in the danger and the furious pace, responding to it with a detached fury of its own.

Jimmy switched his display system back on. The lights didn't matter now, and he needed to keep track of his pursuers. What he saw surprised him. They were pulling back. When Jimmy looked up, he realised why. Only a few hundred metres ahead, the track went into a tunnel. Jimmy was hurtling directly towards the side of a hill.

Pull up, he pleaded with himself. But his body flicked away his fear. *Please*, he begged, battling his own instincts. His body wasn't responding. The ground loomed towards him. Was this part of his programming, he wondered. Perhaps he was destined to destroy himself to avoid capture.

The world seemed to slow down around him. Every clump of mud in the hillside was cast into sharp relief by the floodlights behind. The sharp outline of his own helicopter's shadow grew rougher and rougher, larger and larger. There was nowhere to go. Above and around him was a net of military firepower controlled by NJ7. Ahead of him was solid earth, with no way through.

Through, Jimmy thought. *Of course*. At last he realised what his programming was planning. With split-second timing, Jimmy's hands heaved on the controls. The helicopter slowed momentarily, darted sideways, then charged along the track, directly behind the train.

Jimmy plunged into the tunnel, but the rotors of the chopper were too wide. They snapped off with a powerful crunch and shattered in every direction. Jimmy knew he had no control now. All he could hear was the piercing screech of his runners scraping along the track. In the fountain of sparks, Jimmy saw that the nose of his cabin was pressing against the back of the train.

This was only half the plan. For the rest, he had to move faster than he ever had before. He swung himself out of his seat and around the side of the helicopter. The metal casing was burning hot to the touch, but he wasn't holding it long enough to care. The friction of the tracks was slowing the chopper, while the train powered ahead. Before a gap could open up between them, Jimmy flung himself forwards, pouring all of his strength into stretching for a safe landing.

The back of the train seemed to jump up and smack him in the face. The impact knocked all the wind from his chest. The tips of his fingers caught a metal rim of some part of the carriage, but he couldn't even see what he was clinging on to. Somehow he managed to claw his way round to the side of the train for a firmer grip and closed his eyes against the rush of wind and dust in his face.

The train burst out of the tunnel with the body of the chopper bouncing behind it. Jimmy opened his eyes to see that the whole airborne fleet was there waiting for him. Within a second, the sky was lit up with the blast of rockets. Jimmy gasped and clenched every muscle. He couldn't believe it – NJ7 were actually going to blow up a train full of innocent passengers just to kill him.

But they weren't. Instead, the rockets slammed into the broken and battered helicopter he'd just left. The rotorless body of the chopper erupted into a huge ball of flame. It tumbled along the track, spitting fire and debris in a huge circle around it.

Jimmy rattled on towards London, untouched.

The Cavendish Hotel on London's Jermyn Street offered five-star accommodation from a past era. It was one of the city's oldest remaining independent hotels, but everybody knew it wouldn't survive for long. Hardly any tourists were allowed into the country these days, and there was no reason for British people to come and stay, even if they could afford it. That left only wealthy foreign businessmen, and most of them had better taste than to stay within the Cavendish's sprawling corridors, with its peeling paintwork and lights dim enough to hide the stains on the walls.

More importantly to Zafi Sauvage, the service was erratic. For example, the management team didn't care enough to ask each other about her – the pretty twelve-year-old girl who had recently appeared on the cleaning staff. As long as her uniform was tidy and she appeared busy with something, successive managers each assumed she was on work-experience for somebody else. It was an assumption Zafi nurtured through artful manipulation.

She even had the head concierge believing that she was sixteen, and the daughter of a foreign investor, on an undercover fact-finding mission. It was far-fetched but just about believable. Perhaps more so than the truth. Who would have believed that she was a genetically designed assassin working for the DGSE – the French Secret Service?

Zafi set about polishing the handrail on the main staircase, while she peeked down at the clock in the lobby. It was 4.50 a.m. In ten minutes she knew there would be a shift change and she knew exactly which team would be starting work. Memorising the rota had been one of the first steps in her assimilation on to the staff.

She left the gold of the handrail gleaming and trotted back up to the landing, where a service door took her into the Cavendish's behind-the-scenes labyrinth. The twisting passages and spiral staircases of the ancient building were the perfect place to vanish.

This was just the first stage of Zafi's disappearing act. From here, the whole world could become her labyrinth. Travel documents were easy to come by and easy to copy. Entire false identities could be created while inattentive receptionists took coffee breaks. The kitchens were a bountiful source of supplies and, thanks to the many empty bedrooms, she was well rested. The only question was where to go. Could she ever return to France? Her last mission for the DGSE had gone perfectly until the final moments. Instead of killing her targets, she'd helped them escape.

Zafi pattered through the corridors of the hotel, trying to picture the scenes back in Paris. Did her Secret Service bosses know yet that her targets were still alive? Could they possibly suspect that she'd failed on purpose? She was overcome by a rush of desperation. Would she ever get the chance to prove to them that she could be effective?

Her step was so light on the floorboards that there was hardly a creak. She made it to a storeroom of long-forgotten lost property and snatched up her jacket and a shoulder bag she'd packed full of essentials. In the pocket of her uniform she could feel the outline of her mobile phone, heavy on her skin. She knew the DGSE must have been trying to get in touch, but she didn't dare check her messages.

Zafi slipped out of a fire escape into the back alley behind the hotel. Her timing was perfect. A rubbish truck rumbled into view at the end of the alley. The silhouettes of two burly refuse collectors lumbered towards the back door of the hotel. Zafi skipped past the pile of black plastic sacks and kept to the shadows. She easily slipped past the men without being noticed.

When she reached the truck, she pulled out her phone. It would be so easy to toss it away forever. Her old life would be over – crushed in the back of a rubbish truck. The DGSE would try to track her down, but they'd never find her. She was too good for that. She would let them assume she'd been killed in action by the British.

Her fist squeezed the phone so tightly it almost cracked the plastic casing. But she didn't throw it. Her arm refused to move. She could feel her breath growing short and her limbs tightening. In seconds the rubbish men would be back and her chance would be gone. What was stopping her?

She glanced at the display on her phone. *One new message.* Her imagination dreaded what it might say. She'd failed to complete her mission. They could be recalling her to Paris to receive some kind of punishment. Or perhaps they were already laying a trap for her. Had she turned from France's greatest weapon to an embarrassment, or even an enemy? Zafi gritted her teeth and told herself not to be so dramatic. *It was just a mission*, she thought. *But without a mission, I'm nothing.* In the corner of her eye she could see the rubbish collectors coming back, their backs laden with plastic sacks. Zafi pulled in a deep breath. *I'm an assassin*, she told herself. *I can handle it.* She delicately tapped the buttons on her phone and read the message.

As usual, it was in the form of an encrypted stream of letters and numbers. Zafi relished the warm hum in her brain, allowing her to read the code as simply as if it was a French nursery rhyme. When she saw what it said, the warmth spread from her head to the rest of her body. They obviously didn't know what had happened – and they weren't interested in the details. For now, at least, it looked like they trusted her. Zafi felt a surge of delight. They needed her. Something more pressing had come up and she was to turn her attention to it immediately.

At last Zafi smiled. This would be her chance. Who would care about the past if she completed this new mission? It would be the greatest achievement of any French assassin in history. It was the chance to prove she was still the best. To the DGSE and to herself.

She pulled off her maid's uniform to reveal a thin black tracksuit underneath. She tossed the uniform into the rubbish truck, slipped the phone back into her pocket and set off at a jog. She headed south, towards Westminster. Her new target wouldn't be hard to find.

She'd tried to eliminate him a couple of times before, but on each occasion somebody had been there to stop her. She'd tried to shoot him, but Jimmy Coates had got in the way. Then, more recently, she had intended to poison this target with the raw, untreated meat of a Greenland Shark. An NJ7 operative had ambushed her in Iceland and stopped her getting away with the poisonous meat.

This time Zafi knew she would succeed. She had to. For a short time she had let confusion get in the way of her identity. But she was back. And to prove it to everybody, only one man had to die. The five words of the message drummed through her head: "Terminate the British Prime Minister."

Jimmy couldn't believe that after an explosion like that on the track the train had continued its journey – and without the slightest delay. It was unusual for a train to be on time even without such a catastrophe on the line. He could only assume that NJ7 wanted to keep the little drama secret – as secret as an aerial fire fight and an explosion could be.

Even so, with every shift in the rhythm of the train's rocking and every variation in the regular beat of the journey, Jimmy expected the worst. *They'll search the tunnel and the wreckage*, he told himself. *They'll know I'm alive and that I'm on this train.*

He had found a corner at the end of a carriage where he could sit without being observed. After he'd climbed in through the window he'd found a book that had fallen from one of the baggage racks and now he was leaning against the door to the toilet, pretending to read.

He didn't even see the words on the page. He couldn't settle his eyes on one thing for more than half a second. Nothing in his surroundings changed. Nobody came for him. Yet he couldn't stop his nerves clattering as hard as the train. The cold from the floor crept through his body. He could feel heat spreading from his stomach and knew that his programming was trying to warm him and settle his nerves at the same time, but he fought it.

They're trying to kill me, he told himself. *It's right to be on edge*. The last thing Jimmy wanted to do was relax. He wasn't ready to. His imagination was still replaying the explosion over and over, and his ears were still ringing from the successive booms. Most of all, he could still feel a rage inside him that was bursting to be let out.

At first he thought he was angry at the people who'd tried to blow him up, but slowly he realised that wasn't true. The faceless pilots meant nothing to him, even when they aimed their rockets and pulled the trigger. Jimmy's anger was for their boss. Not just the British Government, but one man. The new Prime Minister. The man who had given the Secret Service greater powers than ever before. The man who had fuelled public fear and hatred of the French to strengthen his own position.

The man who had forced Neo-democracy even deeper into the British system and removed any chance that people might have to vote. The man who had once been Jimmy's father – Ian Coates.

Jimmy had to put his book down and hold his head. He'd never felt such confusion. It was like madness. His hands were shaking violently and he knew now that he had to give in to that inner wash of calm. It dampened all of his emotions, blunting their bite. He concentrated on that inner cloud, cursing himself for resisting his programming. If he was to stay alive, he had to stay focused. And that meant *not* thinking about his father.

Over the past few weeks Jimmy thought he'd learned when to listen to his programming – he'd even been able to control it at times. But it was changing so fast, and it felt like the human in him was changing too. The lines weren't so clear any more. Nothing was clear. He closed his eyes and let his lungs slow his breathing, despite the smell of the nearby toilet. He thought back to all the times when this strange force swelling inside him had saved him, trying to forget that without it he wouldn't have been in trouble in the first place.

But for tonight's crisis, he blamed himself. Why had he hesitated to escape from that newsroom when he knew the police were so close? He'd been stupid to even think that there might be news of his family there. Why would a local newspaper in the south of England have any interest in reporting the fates of three insignificant Londoners? That's even if they'd been allowed to without censorship.

The last Jimmy had heard, his mum, sister and best friend had been in the custody of NJ7. Then the French Secret Service had sent an assassin to kill them, to punish Jimmy when a deal had gone bad. He had no idea what had happened to them after that.

For all Jimmy knew he was completely alone in the world. Right now, the power in his blood was the only ally he had. It could remove the pain of loneliness. It could remove his father from his mind completely. *It's on my side*, he told himself. *It's me*. But at the same he shuddered with terror. If this power inside was him, he was more killer than human.

03 THE WALNUT TREE PROJECT

Mitchell Glenthorne shifted uncomfortably in his seat and his knee twitched under the table. The eyes of everybody in the room seemed to burn into him. He wasn't used to the scrutiny of the most powerful people in the country.

Around the long, lozenge-shaped table were the dozen men and women who could do almost anything they wanted with Great Britain. Thanks to Neo-democracy, they didn't need to worry about the opinions of the British people. They could get on with the efficient day-to-day running of the country, much of which was done from here, the Cabinet Room at Number 10 Downing Street.

But however powerful these people were, they were under the control of a single man – Ian Coates, the Prime Minister. He was sitting at the centre of the table, leaning on his elbows with his shirtsleeves rolled up. Directly behind his head was one of Downing Street's old portraits. Mitchell didn't know who it was, but he recognised the new flag just above – a Union Jack, with an extra green stripe running down the centre. That green stripe was the emblem of NJ7.

"Ladies and gentlemen," Ian Coates announced, "this is Britain's finest asset." It took a second for Mitchell to realise they were still talking about him. "A miracle of British science and genetic engineering." The PM's voice was low and stern. Mitchell wondered whether he spoke quietly on purpose, so that people had to crane their necks and listen closely for every word. He certainly wasn't a charismatic speaker. Usually his imposing physical presence was enough – broad shoulders, thick brown hair and a heavy brow. But today Mitchell noticed the dark bags under his eyes and skin so pale it was almost yellow.

"He's only thirteen years old," the PM continued, "but Mitchell's recent heroism has made Britain stronger, and shown us true British success."

British success? When Mitchell thought back over his missions, all he could remember was the empty ache of failure. He wondered whether that was what the PM meant by "British success".

"Learn from him." The Prime Minister tapped his pen on the table and drew in a deep breath. "I invited him to this meeting because he's an example to *everybody*." Mitchell thought he saw a glimmer of emotion in Ian Coates' bloodshot eyes. It quickly passed. Could the man have been thinking of his son, Mitchell wondered?

Nobody was allowed to mention the fact that for eleven years Ian and Jimmy Coates had lived happily as part of the same family.

"Now we need people like Mitchell more than ever," the PM declared. "We have a new danger."

Let me out of here, Mitchell screamed silently. He longed for a mission, or at least to get back to his simple, disciplined and anonymous life in the underground bunkers of NJ7. It was almost as if the sunlight filtering through the lace curtains carried poison into his skin.

At last the Prime Minister took his eyes off Mitchell. "I've asked William Lee to brief you all," he announced, with a dismissive wave towards the man on Mitchell's right.

"Thank you, Prime Minister." Slowly, the man stood up – and up and up. He was by far the tallest man anybody in the room had ever seen. Mitchell had started to get used to it over the last few days, but clearly several members of the Cabinet were overwhelmed. William Lee towered above them, his shadow running the entire length of the tabletop. Mitchell would have described the man's face as Indian, but he knew that didn't quite capture the unique character of his features: long, thin nose; eyes like black olives.

"Jimmy Coates is alive," Lee began. "He's in Britain and he's spreading misinformation about the Government. Miss Bennett, the file." He turned and looked down at the person on Mitchell's left: the Head of NJ7, the most frightening and beautiful woman Mitchell had ever known. He was barely able to gather the courage to turn and look at her now.

She nodded to Lee with a delicate smile and tossed a manila folder into the centre of the table. Its contents spilled across the lacquer – printouts of web pages, stills of Jimmy's video message, photos of the break-in at the newspaper office in Hailsham, along with reams of other documents and reports.

Mitchell's eyes remained on Miss Bennett. Apart from Mitchell, she was the youngest person in the room. Mitchell guessed she must have been in her late thirties, but with such glowing skin and bright red lipstick she often seemed younger. She looked as she always did – her back straight, her mouth in a knowing half-smile, her chestnut hair pulled back tightly and held in place by a green clip. Yet Mitchell was suspicious. She wouldn't normally have co-operated so readily with William Lee. Mitchell wondered whether at that very moment her assistants were delving into Lee's past in another effort to undermine his position.

Technically, William Lee was nothing more than Director of Special Security for the Prime Minister, but he had quickly won Coates' trust and established himself at the heart of the Government. When he spoke, he had all the authority of a world leader.

"Lies spread fast," he said. "We're following protocol,

which means Miss Bennett has an NJ7 team working with the Corporation as we speak, to shut down any websites that carry his messages and limit the damage. But these lies seem to be spreading more quickly than any we've encountered from any opposition before. We traced the initial breach of information security to the office of a local newspaper in Hailsham. The editor and staff are in custody. They're sharing what they know."

Mitchell couldn't help shuddering. He didn't need to see the pictures in the manila folder. He knew what Lee meant by "sharing what they know". He'd seen the stale bloodstains on the floors of NJ7 interview rooms.

Suddenly Lee was interrupted by a heavy sigh from Miss Bennett. Everybody looked to her.

"Sorry to interrupt," she said, in a way that made it obvious she wasn't sorry at all. "But shouldn't you tell everybody exactly what this boy's saying that's so dangerous?"

Lee responded calmly. "Fine. He's saying that the Government's reasons for going to war with France are based on a lie. He claims we weren't attacked by the French."

"And were we?" Miss Bennett's smile broadened, but her eyes glinted like blades.

"Were we what?"

"Were we attacked by the French? Or were we wrong?"

"Wrong?" Lee snapped. "The evidence was presented, discussed and agreed upon. You were there, and you agreed with the Prime Minister's decision."

"I agreed on the basis of the evidence," Miss Bennett replied. "If it turns out that evidence was misleading, and we have new evidence..."

"The decision to attack France has already been taken," Lee interrupted, "and now we must follow through."

Mitchell tried to shrink into his chair. He was stuck in the middle of the argument. Even though he was secretly delighted that Miss Bennett knew exactly how to infuriate William Lee, he hated having the eyes of the room aimed in his direction again. In desperation he looked to the Prime Minister, hoping he'd put a stop to the discussion. But Coates was staring into the middle distance, his head swaying slightly from side to side. Was he OK, Mitchell wondered?"

"Tell me," Miss Bennett was saying, "have you considered *why* Jimmy Coates's message is spreading more quickly than anti-Government messages have in the past?"

Lee wasn't phased by the question. "I'm sure your team at the Information Division knows much more than I could about which messages people choose to disperse over the Internet." He let out an awkward chuckle. "It seems to me that people will forward any old rubbish. They send all their friends personality quizzes, ridiculous jokes and pictures of monkeys dressed as penguins."

"I haven't seen that picture," Miss Bennett cut in.

"I think I'd like to. Mitchell, make sure I see the penguin-monkey that Mr Lee knows so much about. I don't want to be left behind." Mitchell squirmed. "And find out about 'jokes' as well. I might like them."

"Miss Bennett!" William Lee couldn't help raising his voice now, and looked around the room for support. Mitchell knew that only the Prime Minister would have dared tell Miss Bennett to be quiet and right now he looked far away, concentrating on something else.

"No need to shout," purred Miss Bennett. "All I'm saying is that it looks like people are responding to the boy's message. Maybe they believe him, and maybe they *want* to believe him."

Mitchell was amazed. He'd seen Miss Bennett argue with William Lee before, but never in front of so many other people.

"A message doesn't spread itself, does it?" she went on. "It takes members of the public to—"

"Members of the public?" roared Ian Coates, suddenly bursting into life as if he'd just woken up from a nightmare. Everybody was startled. "Since when did we take the advice of strangers in the street on how to run the country?"

Mitchell watched the faces of Miss Bennett and William Lee. They were both dumbfounded by Ian Coates' outburst. But as the PM went on, Mitchell noticed a change in his voice. It was thin and frail, like the voice of a man thirty years older.

"Members of the public?!" Coates repeated, even more indignant. "The system of Neo-democracy protects the British people from the ignorance of the general population." His eyes bulged with rage and his temples were throbbing. Mitchell found he couldn't look away from the beads of sweat glistening in the furrows on the man's forehead. "The vital decisions are taken by experts," Coates was saying. "By *us*. Nobody in Britain should live with the responsibility that they might have to make decisions of national importance. The consequences of such decisions are immense."

Around the table, the Cabinet members were either staring into their laps or shooting each other glances of concern at the Prime Minister's outburst. But nobody dared interrupt him.

"It is more vital than ever," he went on, "that the country is fully behind this Government. The war with France is a vital part of that process. It's the perfect way to unite everybody in Britain. And we'll be united behind Neo-democracy." He fixed his glare on William Lee. "That's why we've come up with the Walnut Tree Project." With another curt wave, he indicated that Lee should continue the briefing.

"Quite simply," Lee explained, still rattled by the PM's rant, "we have planned a new French attack. Not a strike on an oil rig or military target, but an attack on the British people themselves. This will be the best reminder to everybody in the country that we have a common enemy."

"You're going to attack British citizens yourself and then blame the French?" Miss Bennett wasn't aghast, as Mitchell expected her to be. She sounded like she was calmly clarifying the details.

"We'll try to minimise casualties, of course," Lee replied. "But for the attack to look genuine, some members of society may have to be sacrificed."

"Expendable ones," Coates explained. "Criminals the courts haven't convicted yet, homeless people, the unemployable..."

"I've chosen the most suitable site I could find on such short notice," said William Lee. He picked up a large roll of paper from the floor and unfurled it on the table. It was a map of London. "In order to have the most impact, I realised that it had to be somewhere in London. And then I thought – why not use this to solve our other little problem?"

Everybody looked puzzled. Mitchell already suspected what Lee had in mind before he explained, "Jimmy Coates escaped our aerial task force. The strike on his helicopter was a success, but it turns out Jimmy wasn't in it."

Sounds like a British success, Mitchell thought to himself.

"Our investigative team now believes he could only have slipped away on the train. The train reached London twenty minutes ago, making it too late to seal Waterloo Station. But if we stage the attack carefully, in the vicinity of Waterloo, and we clear the area of police and ordinary security services, we might be able to tempt Jimmy Coates out of hiding to try to stop the explosion. We'll make sure he doesn't succeed, of course. At the very least, we may be able to pick up his trail. With any luck we'll blow him up along with the building."

Finally, Lee leaned forward, his shadow extending over the map of London like night falling across the city. He extended an elegant index finger and tapped a small lane called Walnut Tree Walk in Lambeth. All he said was, "A tower block."

Everybody craned forward to get a look at the exact spot. The people at the far end of the table had to stand up to see and a general murmur broke out. Mitchell waited for someone to make an objection, but from the fear on their faces it was obvious nobody was going to. He wondered whether he should protest himself, but when he took a breath to speak it seemed to freeze his throat. He looked again at the map. The lines swirled around with the confusion in his head. He didn't understand the politics of it, but he understood that the Government was going to blow up its own people just so they could blame the French.

"It's for the greater good," Lee whispered, resting a hand on Mitchell's shoulder. Mitchell quickly nodded and made his face go blank. It wasn't his job to react to Government decisions. He was lucky to even be at this meeting.

"Prime Minister."

A firm voice broke through the hubbub. It was Miss Bennett. Her icy tone forced everybody back into their seats and commanded their attention. "Clearly you won't be dissuaded from this ridiculous plot, and I can see the logic in it, but I must urge you not to rush into this. A disaster like this will certainly pull the country together and distract people from Internet rumours, but it does seem a little... clumsy."

"Clumsy?" barked Coates.

"Yes. Like sending a torpedo to kill a mosquito."

"It would do the job," mumbled William Lee.

"It would also do the job to give an NJ7 team a little more time to shut down or reframe the necessary websites and spread counter-information. Meanwhile we'll continue to hunt Jimmy Coates. We know he's in London. There isn't a square millimetre of the city that's not covered by cameras or real-time satellite imaging – or both. We'll find him and kill him by the end of the day."

"A day is too long," Coates rasped. "The operation is already under way."

"I thought you'd say that." Miss Bennett shrugged. "So my objections are over-ruled?" The Prime Minister nodded. With a flourish, Miss Bennett unclipped her hair and let it tumble about her shoulders. She tapped her hairclip on the table and with a broad smile announced, "You're a fool."

There was general shock around the table, but Ian Coates looked close to smiling too.

"We're blowing up a tower block," he insisted quietly. Then he pounded his fist on the table and roared, "We're blowing up the tower block on Walnut Tree Walk! If anybody has any problem with that they can leave the room now!"

Mitchell looked up and down the table. Nobody made eye contact. The only noise was the soft shuffle of people shifting in their seats. Mitchell knew that if anybody left the room now they would never make it to the street. Miss Bennett was simply watching calmly. The Prime Minister broke the silence.

"We all agree that Neo-democratic principles are vital to the strength of this country, don't we?" There was a reserved murmur of agreement from his Cabinet. "And that it is our duty to protect Neo-democracy whenever it is threatened." Again, people nodded and muttered, slightly louder this time.

"Then the British public has nothing to fear from the people in this room. We're protecting them." Coates' voice rose steadily and started to quiver. "The danger comes from beyond Britain's boundaries. If people don't know that then it's our duty to show them." He pushed himself to his feet and supported himself on the table. "Their fear will protect the system, and it's the system which is protecting them. If they question the system then they're not afraid enough!" Mitchell watched, astounded, as the Prime Minister swayed more violently, then staggered backwards, knocking his chair to the floor. "Don't they realise there's a foreign country only thirty-six kilometres away across the English Channel, and that it's full of French people?!" The PM was staggering about now, blinking frantically and unable to balance himself. Every member of the Cabinet, except Miss Bennett and William Lee, rushed to try and support him. Like a feverish bear, he swiped them away.

"There are horrors on our doorstep!" he wailed, his words slurring into each other. "If people are sleeping so soundly at night that they can spread the cankerous filth of an ignorant, traitorous boy..." He rocked to one side and threw his arm out towards the mantelpiece to catch himself, but missed and sent a huge vase crashing to the floor.

Suddenly, people were rushing everywhere to the sounds of screams and desperate shouts for help. Mitchell was transfixed. He felt like he was watching everything in slow motion: the Prime Minister's eyes rolled back in his head. His arms shuddered and his upper body twisted like a snowflake in the wind. Finally, his legs seemed to melt away from under him. He swivelled and collapsed forwards on to the table, smashing his forehead into the wood. His outstretched fingertips were centimetres from Miss Bennett's hairclip.

04 CRATE EXPECTATIONS

Jimmy hurried away from Waterloo Station. It hadn't been hard for him to stay unnoticed by the commuters bustling their way to work. They kept their grim faces downcast unless they were squinting up at the departures board. Jimmy was more worried about keeping his face off the surveillance cameras. With facial recognition software, he'd be picked out of the crowd in seconds.

Fortunately, that also worked in his favour. It meant that nobody would be monitoring the camera feeds personally, and there was no software that knew to look out for a boy wandering through the streets alone.

On the train journey he'd managed to find out a little more vital information from a leaflet he'd found behind the snack bar. It was the train operator's guidelines on emergency procedures, and it confirmed what he'd thought: the only major hospitals left in the country were in the big cities. It set out clearly that in the case of a significant incident at Waterloo, the nearest hospital with the facilities to cope was a place called St Thomas'.

Jimmy didn't want to risk going anywhere else. If the other hospitals weren't big enough or well enough funded to cope with more than a few casualties, there was no way they'd be any help with Jimmy's radiation poisoning. He'd be putting himself in danger for nothing. No – he had one shot at going to a hospital so it had to work. It had to be St Thomas'.

Jimmy had only been to hospital once before, and he'd been too young to remember now which hospital it had been. He'd fallen in an adventure playground and his mum thought he'd broken his arm, so she'd taken him for an x-ray.

All Jimmy remembered was sitting in the waiting room for hours and hours, only to be told that he was fine. It was almost funny now to think of the way his body had developed. Since his powers had kicked in, it took a lot more than falling down to break his arm. All those cuts and bruises he'd suffered while he was growing up – those days were over. Jimmy knew that it was extreme danger that had awakened his programming early, but he wondered whether there was anything that could possibly make it go away again. He quickly told himself to put thoughts of the impossible out of his mind. His programming couldn't be switched off. It was part of him.

Jimmy prowled through the streets towards the River Thames. He reckoned the streets were safer that the tunnels of the Underground system, and he'd memorised the map from the train leaflet to guide him to St Thomas'. But within minutes he saw that he had a problem. Armed policemen were blockading the roads and pavements.

Jimmy slipped into the doorway of a café to hide, feeling a surge of anger at himself. How could he have hoped to walk to the hospital? *They've already set up a ring round the station*, Jimmy realised. He'd been counting on it taking a little longer for NJ7 to work out he'd been on the train, not in the wreckage of the helicopter.

There was nothing for it but to turn round and walk back in the direction he'd come. Retracing his steps increased his chances of being recognised, so he chose a different route, while still making his way back towards Waterloo Station. All the time, he was racking his brains. If he couldn't get to the hospital on foot, it was obvious NJ7 would have the Underground platforms monitored as well – that's if the trains were running at all.

By now Jimmy was feeling like every thought had to fight its way through a veil of tiredness and hunger. He didn't dare try to remember the last time he'd slept for more than a couple of hours at a time, and his stomach was aching for some kind of breakfast.

Very soon he was back in the network of road tunnels around Waterloo Station. *If they've set up a ring*, he thought to himself, *I'm safest in the centre*. He could feel frustration biting at the back of his mind.

He didn't have any time to waste, yet it looked like the only thing he could do was wait. His programming was throbbing through his brain, like dark liquid coating the inside of his skull. It was lining up his options: surely NJ7 wouldn't be checking the boot of every car, would they? What about the undercarriages?

Jimmy rounded a corner and realised that his body had subconsciously guided him to one of the station's service entrances. He moved without hesitation, keeping his head ducked low behind the mounds of discarded plastic crates. This was where the stock was delivered to the retail and refreshment outlets. It was a little late for a delivery, but if any supply lorry had been held up it could provide Jimmy with two things: a much needed breakfast and a potential escape opportunity.

Within seconds, Jimmy's prayers were answered. A white van swung into one of the bays. It backed up to a set of loading doors and stopped. Jimmy waited for the driver to get out. He'd have to choose his moment carefully. What was in the van, he wondered. Sandwiches? Crisps? Muffins? There was nothing on the van that gave any clue – no writing, no logo... But Jimmy's chance to find out didn't come.

The van simply waited for about a minute, then pulled off again. Jimmy let out a soft grunt of annoyance. His stomach turned over. Why on earth would a van pull up, wait, then pull off again? It didn't matter. Jimmy had a choice: find a way into the station through the doors and swipe some food, or wait here for another van to show up. He wasn't in a waiting mood.

Checking the positions of all the security cameras, Jimmy crept out from his hiding place. He had to move slowly, letting his inner voice guide him through the lines of sight of all the cameras as they swivelled. He was only a few steps from the doors when he heard the squeak of old brakes. In an instant he dived behind another pile of crates, just in time to watch the same white van return to the bay it had left barely minutes before. Jimmy hunched low, peering between the plastic slats. Now he was intrigued.

Again, the van did nothing but sit there for about sixty seconds before roaring off. This time Jimmy didn't move. Instead he counted. He couldn't help it. A part of him longed to get into the back of the station and keep moving. But his programming froze his limbs and wouldn't let them budge. After three minutes his patience was rewarded. The van returned.

Jimmy tried to get a look at the driver, but he couldn't see past the reflection on the window before the van drove off again, only to be back three minutes later. *It must be circling the station*, Jimmy realised. But why? Was it some kind of signal? Was the driver waiting for instructions? Was he looking for someone? Jimmy couldn't help wondering whether this van was part of the operation that was searching for him. But that didn't feel right. Why would NJ7 have a single white van circling the station and returning to the same bay every few minutes?

The mystery only deepened when the van next returned. This time the driver gave two short blasts on the horn. Two well-built men in grimy blue overalls emerged from the station and immediately flung open the back of the van. Then they started loading it with crates, which were all either sealed or covered in grey blankets. As the first one emerged from the darkness of the station, Jimmy's skin prickled, but he didn't know why. He peered more closely at the crates.

They were obviously very heavy and the men were taking great care handling them. They wore huge gloves and set each crate down in the van like they were putting a baby to bed. Jimmy wanted to creep closer to work out what was going on. Something inside him seemed to be drawing him forwards. He took a deep breath to calm himself, but it only intensified the feeling. Then he realised why: it was something in the air.

Nitroglycerin.

The word seemed to lurk in his brain without him realising how it got there. It was as if he'd breathed it in. At first he wasn't even sure what it meant, but then a low hum vibrated through his body, bringing with it a frightening certainty: highly volatile explosive.

Felix Muzbeke opened his mouth as wide as it would go – which was wider than most – and in a single bite consumed more than half a bagel.

"You're disgusting," said Georgie Coates softly.

Felix grinned, which allowed a strand of pastrami to escape his lips and hang from the corner of his mouth.

"How come you're not fat?" Georgie asked, chomping down on her own bagel. Felix shrugged and kept chewing. A businessman shoved past them to reach the front of the queue so Felix and Georgie hurried out of the way and back on to the main concourse of London Bridge Station.

"What is it about Chris and stations?" Felix asked, once his mouth was at last free of bagel. "We're going to spend the rest of our lives hiding in underground passages."

"They're good places to hide, I guess," replied Georgie. "We don't exactly want Miss Bennett to be able to drop in any time she likes. Chris is the Government's biggest enemy."

"Apart from Jimmy," added Felix, with a hint of pride.

"Maybe."

Georgie's eyes were constantly scanning the faces of everybody else in the station. Any of the security staff could be looking for them, acting on instructions from NJ7. Any of the commuters could be plain-clothes security staff.

Meanwhile, Felix watched Georgie carefully. She was paying more attention to the surroundings than she was to her bagel. Every now and again Felix wondered whether she might have hidden inside her some of the same powers that Jimmy had. Perhaps she just hadn't discovered them yet. Felix didn't dare to ask, but he was amazed at how well Georgie adapted to this life of hiding, of constantly monitoring everybody around her, of surviving on station food when every journey in public was a potential death trap. He felt almost as reassured being with her as he would have with Jimmy. Plus, there was the chance that she wouldn't finish her bagel and he'd get the leftovers.

"Come on," said Georgie firmly, "we'd better get back. We've been in the open too long already." They hurried across the station forecourt.

"It's not my fault," replied Felix. "They took ages to make my bagel."

"Next time just have something normal. You know, from the shelf."

"What's wrong with pastrami and pineapple?" Felix polished off the last bite with a grin and took Georgie's bottle of smoothie from her hand.

"Hey!" she protested.

"Just a sip."

"OK, but drink with your head down." Georgie flicked her eyes towards the security cameras. Felix struggled to drink from the bottle while keeping his face turned towards the floor.

"Do you think Jimmy can drink without moving his head?" he asked.

"Most people can drink without moving their..." Georgie turned to see that Felix had ended up with a dribble of smoothie down his chin. "OK," she corrected herself. "Most sane people."

Felix wiped his mouth and couldn't help chuckling. He'd never imagined that he'd end up being such close friends with Georgie. Not only was she a girl, but she was two years older than him. Despite that, it didn't feel weird. There was nobody else for him to spend time with. No school, no socialising... *No family*, he thought. He felt a chill run through his bones. The idea crept up on him without warning.

Felix's parents had been seized in New York by men who looked like NJ7 agents. They hadn't been seen since. But they were constantly on Felix's mind, on the edge of every thought. He used to think he'd seen them every time he was in a crowd of people, but such illusions quickly faded. He couldn't let the hope that he would see them again do the same.

"Hey," he said brightly, trying to distract himself, "what do you think Jimmy feels like when he's doing all that stuff?"

"What stuff?" Georgie asked. "You mean his..." She dropped her voice and whispered, "Powers?"

"Do you think it's like an electric shock?" Felix wondered aloud. "Or like a hot shower?"

"Oh, I would *so* love a hot shower," Georgie groaned.

"He could have so much fun," Felix went on. "I mean, you know, if people weren't trying to kill him and everything."

"If you ask me, his powers are useless," said Georgie quickly. "He could be the strongest boy on Earth, but he still wouldn't be able to change the Government."

"He probably *is* the strongest boy on Earth," Felix pointed out. "Except for Mitchell maybe. But he's not just strong. What about everything else? Can you imagine it? He could call a bank and make his voice sound like the bank manager and tell them to pay him millions of pounds. He's probably living in luxury somewhere. He could—"

"I don't think banks work like that," Georgie pointed out. "And since when could Jimmy imitate voices?"

"He can," Felix insisted. "He told me. I bet he can fly too."

"How are you such an idiot?" Georgie sighed, unable to hide the smile on her face.

"Natural talent," Felix beamed. "You finishing that bagel?"

Jimmy's programming was in control, processing the world around him by breaking it down into millions of tiny pieces of information — including the scent of every chemical in the air. He picked them apart like flavours: diesel fuel, stale bread, rotting vegetables, sweat, cats... and hundreds of other things.

He had never been able to do this before. His programming was growing, developing all the time. The realisation made him shiver. He longed to shut off his senses, almost wishing his own skull could collapse in on itself to squeeze the thoughts out of his head.

The slamming of the van doors jerked Jimmy back to

reality. By the time he had come to his senses, the van was pulling away. Jimmy wanted to feel relieved. Whatever was in those crates, it was gone now and nothing to do with him.

Yet all Jimmy could hear were the doubts circling in his head. They spiralled together and grew into a thumping determination that overpowered every other emotion. Once he'd caught the scent of nitroglycerin, the assassin in him couldn't let it go. The odour brought with it snippets of information locked in his brain. He never realised he knew anything about explosives, but now he could feel it. And the feeling was telling him that nitroglycerin was bad news.

It wasn't used in construction or ordinary demolition. *Too unstable*, Jimmy heard in his head. *Hard to control.* There had to be a very special reason why that van's load included nitroglycerin, and Jimmy had a strong suspicion it wasn't to throw a fireworks party. He had to follow that van.

Making sure the other men had gone back into the station, he reached down to the bottom of the pile of crates in front of him. Supporting them was the platform used to move them around – a small wooden square on metal wheels. With a sharp jerk, Jimmy snatched it out from under the crates, which came clattering down to the tarmac. Before the noise had even started, Jimmy was already hurtling away.

When he reached the road he jumped up and threw

the platform under his feet to use it like a skateboard. He landed with a bang and the small metal wheels growled on the pavement. Jimmy could see the back of the van rounding the corner. He pushed off hard against the ground to speed up, but he knew he would never catch up at this rate. With a delicate twist of his knee, he turned into the road, ducked low and caught the back of a passing car.

The exhaust fumes made his head swim and the car behind honked furiously. Jimmy didn't care. He steadily moved hand over hand towards the front of the car, even while it was shifting through the traffic. Jimmy kept his eyes firmly on the back of the van, four or five vehicles ahead. He rode every bump in the street's surface like a snowboarder across ice, keeping his head below the level of the car windows.

The traffic picked up speed now, but even at fifty or sixty kilometres per hour, Jimmy managed to push himself off the front of the first car and catch the back of the next. Again, he clawed his way forwards, until he was close enough to see the face of the front seat passenger in the wing mirror. After only a couple of minutes, the van turned into a side road. Jimmy gently guided himself in the same direction, letting go of the car and taking back control of his own navigation. He ignored that meek inner voice telling him he had no idea what he was expecting to do or find.

It was a fairly quiet street, with large housing estates

on either side of the road. Jimmy hung back. There was no other traffic to hide behind now. About a hundred and fifty metres down the road the van turned off into a driveway. Jimmy lost sight of it and had to hurry forwards. He was just in time see the van disappearing down a ramp into the underground car park beneath a residential tower block.

Then the shadows were lit up by a flash. A loud crack followed almost immediately. Jimmy shuddered. Was that a gunshot? He jumped off his makeshift skateboard and ran down the street. The noise of the world seemed to drop away – the traffic on surrounding streets, the shouts of children in the playground between the estates, a TV game show blaring out from an open window in the tower block itself. All Jimmy could hear was the echo of that single gunshot mixing with his feet pounding the pavement.

Just as Jimmy reached the ramp leading down to the car park he was nearly knocked off his feet. From under the tower block came a moped, roaring into street. The driver's face was covered by a black helmet, but Jimmy recognised the blue overalls. It was the van driver, speeding off up the street.

Jimmy froze. He looked back down the ramp. A solid metal shutter was dropping into place to seal the car park. He turned to look up the street. The moped had disappeared. Jimmy felt a surge of warmth in his legs. They unlocked and thrust Jimmy forwards – but not after the moped. Instead, he dashed down the short slope and dropped into a roll to slip underneath the metal shutter just before it reached the ground.

His programming was telling him one thing: that underneath this building there were crates of nitroglycerin hidden in the back of a van. And somebody had just been shot. Jimmy didn't know why, and he didn't know how he'd stumbled on all of this, but there was no way he could leave it alone.

Of course, Jimmy also had no way of knowing that NJ7 had hoped he would find the van. The driver had followed his instructions to circle Waterloo Station and attract attention with obviously suspicious movements. NJ7 had struck lucky. They might not have been able to find Jimmy, but they'd done the next best thing. They'd drawn him in and trapped him in Walnut Tree Walk.

05 TURNING UP THE HEAT

The metal shutter slammed down on to the concrete, cutting off the last sliver of daylight and sealing Jimmy in the car park. Strip lights cast soft shadows around the rows of cars, lined up between huge supporting pillars. Jimmy stood up and dusted himself off, but the first thing he saw made him feel like his knees would give way.

Next to the entrance was the security attendant's booth. A cup of tea was perched on the ledge inside, still steaming. But the only thing left of the attendant was an explosion of blood and brains on the back wall.

Jimmy staggered back from the booth, clutching at his mouth and nose, as if he could block out the stench of fresh blood. After a second his insides swirled with the force of his programming. It gushed up through his body, blasting away the shock, but it was too late to stop Jimmy retching up the measly contents of his stomach.

Suddenly, the curiosity that had brought him here took on a fierce urgency. While a part of him wanted to curl up in the corner and catch his breath, he knew that wasn't an option. Instead, Jimmy found the guard's phone and walkie-talkie. Both had been smashed – presumably by the same man who had blasted the attendant's head off.

He drove past me on that moped, Jimmy realised, the sickness rising up inside him again. *I could have stopped him.* He felt dizzy, but his programming seemed to crank up a gear. It was like a belt fastening a notch tighter inside his skin, pulling his thoughts into calm, emotionless order.

First he found the van. That wasn't hard – it was parked in the central row, right next to one of the pillars. The rear doors were locked, but Jimmy jabbed his elbow into the catch. There was nothing he could do to help the attendant now, but if he was right about the van containing explosives he had to warn somebody.

He pulled the van doors open and saw that the vehicle was completely full of crates, stacked up three high and covered in a thick grey blanket. When he pulled back the corner of the blanket, he nearly threw up again at what he saw. There were dozens of crates and every single one was packed with slim glass tubes of a clear, jelly-like substance, all connected by a network of black wires. The whole van was one giant bomb.

Jimmy wanted to warn people. He thought of all the residents in the tower above him, of the children in the playground alongside the building. They all had to evacuate. But Jimmy's feet wouldn't run. Instead he remained rooted to the spot while his eyes darted around the contraption in front of him. He traced the lines of wire like he was following the map of a labyrinth, examining the piles, counting precious seconds. How long did he have before it blew up?

Come on, Jimmy told himself, feeling the sweat crawling down his neck. *There's no way you can defuse a bomb.* There was no ticking clock, no red digits showing him a countdown. There certainly wasn't anything that looked like an off switch, and all the wires were the same colour – black. Then he noticed the condensation on the glass tubes.

Of course, he thought. *Nitro freezes at thirteen degrees.* The chemical was usually a liquid, but Jimmy realised it had been cooled into a solid to make it easier to transport. At the same time, he knew that as nitroglycerin thawed, it became even more unstable.

The piles of crates in front of him seemed to change shape. In Jimmy's imagination, some of them even became transparent. He could see exactly how this bomb was supposed to work.

To his horror, he felt a rush of pleasure. Something inside him was impressed by the artful construction of the bomb – thrilled even. It was built in such a way that it required only a single detonator. That would shoot a charge through the wires, setting off a chain reaction as it raised the temperature of each tube of nitroglycerin to melt them in a specific order. That delicately arranged chain reaction would multiply the size of the explosion a hundred times.

The beauty of it was that the bomb was virtually sabotage-proof. The detonator was nowhere to be seen – presumably hidden at the very centre of the pile of crates. Jimmy noticed tiny gold rings round the connections between the wires and the glass tubes. *A second trigger mechanism*, he realised. Any attempt to disconnect the wires or get to the detonator would set off the chain reaction early. That left no way of stopping it, and no way of predicting when it would explode, even with the expertise of an assassin inside him. Jimmy knew this bomb could blow up at any moment.

He ran back and heaved on the metal shutter at the entrance, gritting his teeth and straining every muscle from his neck to his calves. It wouldn't budge. Jimmy fell back, panting. He didn't understand it. In the past, he'd busted through reinforced walls at embassies and Secret Service facilities – why did a residential tower block need protection that was even stronger? He went to the attendant's booth to find the controls. The desk was dripping with blood. Jimmy forced himself to wipe it away. Thick chunks of hot, quivering flesh came with it. But it was useless; the controls did nothing.

With a wild grunt of horror, Jimmy threw himself at the metal shutter once more. He kicked at it and wiped his hands all over it, clawing madly until the grey was smeared with dark red, and shouting out for help. None came. When Jimmy finally stepped away, his chest was heaving and his mind was frantic. There had to be another way out.

He ran to the other side of the car park, to the door that led on to the stairwell that served the flats. Jimmy opened it with an impatient tug, but then had to stop dead. The doorway was blocked, floor to ceiling, by construction rubble.

Jimmy stared at the huge rocks and metal rods that barred his exit and kicked out. He managed to knock the corner off one of the rocks, but it only revealed another layer of rubble behind it. Jimmy knew he didn't have enough time to claw his way out, even if that was possible. As a final attempt to attract the attention of the outside world, he punched his palm into the fire alarm. There were no bells, no sirens.

Jimmy's rising anger mixed with a cold fear. His hands wanted to tremble, but his inner strength held them rigid. Who were the men who'd assembled the bomb and brought it here? Who were they working for? What was it about this particular tower block?

Jimmy closed his eyes for a second to settle himself, then strode back across the concrete towards the white van. As soon as he stood in front of the open van doors again, he sensed a change. The condensation on the glass tubes was disappearing. When Jimmy held his palms up towards the crates he could feel they were slightly warmer than before. *That's the detonating mechanism*, Jimmy realised. He didn't know whether he'd worked it out himself or if it was his programming. The line between the two was constantly blurring.

Now when he looked across the crates, he imagined he could see right to the heart, where he knew there must be a simple heating system. There was no need for a timer or remote signal because as soon as the heater reached a certain temperature, the explosives at the core would become unstable, setting off the chain reaction through the wires and blowing the entire tower block out of existence.

He desperately looked around him, thinking that perhaps if he could find enough water, dousing the crates would dampen the explosion. But in truth he had no idea whether water would have any effect, and there wasn't any to be seen anyway.

The only liquid around was petrol – lots of it. Could Jimmy possibly use that to lessen the force of the explosion? It seemed crazy, but if he was right about how the bomb was designed...

Jimmy dashed back to the attendant's booth and picked up the man's blood-soaked newspaper. He took it to the van and held it against the driver's window, then jabbed his elbow into it hard. He leaned in through the shattered glass to release the hand brake, then he walked to the front of the vehicle and, as carefully as he possibly could, he heaved on the bumper to pull it out of its bay. If this bomb was going to explode, Jimmy thought, he may as well use it to blast through the metal shutter.

It was difficult to move the van at first, and Jimmy didn't want to pull too hard in case he rocked the thawing nitro, but he reasoned that if it had been stable enough to drive through the streets of London, tugging it a few more metres was worth the risk. He took the strain in his back and thighs, then jumped back to the driver's door to push and steer at the same time. Eventually the van was right up against the metal shutter.

Jimmy wiped the sweat from his face with his sleeve. The van was giving off more heat now. He could feel it a metre away. *It won't hold much longer*, Jimmy thought. Now came the harder part. Jimmy grabbed the mug of tea from the attendant's booth. It was still steaming and spattered with blood. Jimmy smashed it against the wall and used the handle to prise open the van's fuel cap.

By now, even the outside of the van was warm to the touch. Jimmy could feel it matched by the rising heat of his own fear. Even if his plan worked, he would only be able to reduce the power of the blast, not prevent it completely. That left a worrying question: Jimmy might stop the whole building collapsing, but how was he going to survive himself?

He went back to the front of the van and tore into the cushion of the driver's seat, pulling out a whole spring and great fistfuls of wadding. He twisted the wadding tight around the spring, leaving a length of metal at the end for him to hold. When he finished he admired his creation: a huge, mouldy candyfloss stick that smelled of damp. Then he pushed the padding into the van's fuel tank, feeding it down as far as he could, and held it there to soak up some diesel.

When he pulled it out a waft of fumes smacked him in the face. It combined with the scent of nitroglycerin already lining his nostrils and set off alarm bells in his head. Was this really a good idea? He gulped, gathered his courage and returned to the bomb.

Using his twist of seat-padding like a paintbrush, Jimmy carefully dabbed the wires with diesel. Despite his nerves, his hand was rock steady. When he leaned in to get to the wires towards the back, his cheek was millimetres from the glass tubes. The heat was much stronger now, making Jimmy sweat harder. Any second, the nitro could reach flashpoint – but Jimmy planned to give it a helping hand.

He dashed back to the attendant's booth and quickly saw what he needed: hooked on to the security guard's belt was a torch. Jimmy wiped the blood from the handle and unscrewed the plastic cap on the front of the flashlight as he ran across the car park.

Now he was a few metres away from the back of the van staring at the enormous bomb in front of him. *What am I doing?* he thought to himself desperately. *I've covered a giant bomb in diesel.* At the same time, his thumb clicked the torch on and off, itching to connect the bare filament with the diesel fumes. Jimmy could feel the battle raging inside him. His familiar, rational terror was obliterated by a wash of something else – something close to joy. His programming was thriving on the heat and the danger, relishing the chance to set off a massive explosion. *Not just set it off*, Jimmy reassured himself. *Control it.*

He knew that lighting the diesel would raise the temperature of the bomb by the critical few degrees needed to set off the blast. But in the seconds before that happened, the flames would burn through the wires, eliminating the delicately designed chain reaction. The crates of nitroglycerin would go up separately and randomly – not as one huge, coordinated eruption.

Finally, Jimmy brought the torch up to the seat stuffing soaked in diesel. He carefully clicked the torch and a spark lit a couple of strands of cotton at the very tip. Immediately, the fumes ignited and the whole twist of material became a flaming beacon.

He stared into the back of the van again. This time the flickering of his flame made the glass tubes seem to dance, as if they were excited about what Jimmy was about to do. *This could be the biggest mistake of my life*, Jimmy thought.

Just do it, he ordered himself. With that, he hurled the flame towards the bomb, twisted on his heels, and ran.

06 *NELSON'S SHADOW*

BANG!

Jimmy was lifted off his feet. The heat stabbed into his back and the whole world disappeared in a white flash. He slammed into the wall at the far end of the car park and slumped to the floor, his brain juddering in his skull.

He rolled for cover behind a car to watch each tube of nitroglycerin roar harder and hotter than the last one. Between blasts, Jimmy caught glimpses of flames melting the insides of cars. The fire spread, buckling the metal of every vehicle until its own petrol tank gave way and added an extra explosion. Jimmy hardly noticed that he was choking back the black smoke. He was fixated on a single thought: had he succeeded? The chain reaction would have blown the whole tower block to pieces in a single blast. Compared to that, this was a minor accident.

Then came an explosion so strong Jimmy felt like it would crack his eyeballs. It sent a rumble through his whole body, juddering his bones and mashing his organs.

For a few seconds he couldn't breathe. He realised the wall behind him was trembling – badly. So was the floor. When Jimmy looked through the chaos he could see the pillars that supported the ceiling were crumbling.

At first, small cracks opened up in the concrete, then chips of it came away and the cracks grew. Jimmy watched, aghast, as a huge cloud of grey dust mixed with the fire and black smoke. *I've got to get out of here*, he thought. But the only way out was through the exit where Jimmy had dragged the van. The metal shutter had been blown to smithereens with the first explosion, so that wasn't a problem any more. But to get out, Jimmy had to run straight past the bomb – while the crates of nitroglycerin were still blowing up.

There was hardly any gap between explosions now. The heat was too great and the thaw was too rapid for any of the nitro to hold. Blast upon blast rocked the whole place. Jimmy staggered to his feet, almost knocked down every time another detonation sent shockwaves through the floor. Concrete rained down around him. He couldn't see anything more than a metre in front of him, he could only hear the explosions and feel the impact. He felt his inner sense trying to time his run, but surely that wasn't possible.

Half sprinting, half stumbling, Jimmy strained forwards with a flood of excitement. *I can make it*, he told himself.

BOOM!

Jimmy was flung into the sky by a pressure wave travelling at 9000 metres per second. The world swirled into an orange and black blur of flame and smoke. All he could feel was pure heat all around him, as if it was coming from his skin itself. Jimmy was thrown across the street inside a massive fireball. Then he slammed against something hard, and although the orange around him disappeared, he still felt like he was on fire. He heard a cry and realised it was his own voice, mixing with hundreds of other peoples' screams.

He felt his body trying to stand, but he couldn't. The last thing he saw was the huge tower block he'd just escaped. One side of it was crumbling, then it slumped downwards and collapsed.

The traffic around Trafalgar Square was even worse than usual. Cars honked and buses snorted as they stacked up in all the surrounding roads. In the very centre of the noise, in the pedestrianised part of the square, a tall, slim man in a long, navy coat was standing on top of an upturned plastic box, a megaphone to his mouth.

"My name is Christopher Viggo," he announced, drawing the attention of a small crowd. "Perhaps you've seen me on the news, and if you believe what you've been told, I'm an enemy of Britain." He paused to make way for a confused murmur. "So I've come here to tell you what's really going on in this country – and what you can do about it!"

He spoke like a true leader, with controlled passion in every word and every movement. Georgie and Felix watched nervously at the edge of the crowd.

"There should be more people," Felix muttered.

"There will be," Georgie reassured him. "Look, they're coming to see what's going on."

She was cut off by her mother, Helen Coates.

"Get among the crowd," she told her daughter. "Before they go anywhere. Take these and give them out." She handed her daughter a box of leaflets then hugged her coat close to her. "You too, Felix." As she spoke she looked anxiously around the square. "Put them into people's pockets if they won't take them."

Before Georgie or Felix could respond, Helen hurried back to stand by Christopher Viggo, whose speech was gaining momentum – and a bigger audience with every passing minute.

"Does Chris think he's going to beat NJ7 with leaflets?" muttered Felix, taking a fistful from the box in Georgie's hand.

"He'll have to if people can't hear what he's saying." Georgie rushed up to a woman standing a couple of metres from Viggo's makeshift stage. "What's going on with this traffic?" Georgie asked. "Nobody can hear Chris."

She was talking to Saffron Walden, Christopher Viggo's girlfriend and a partner in all his campaigning.

She was jumping from foot to foot to keep warm. A woolly hat covered her head and her coat collar was turned up, so between them only her eyes were visible – two hazel jewels shining out against her dark black skin.

"The traffic's only going to get worse," she explained. "Apparently there are road blocks around Waterloo. Nobody seems to know why."

"In that case," said Georgie, "Chris either needs to shout louder or we should find a different spot."

"Looks like we should be moving on anyway." Saffron's eyes flicked to the far side of the square, where a camera crew had appeared. "Once the cameras arrive, the police aren't far behind."

"Will they put Chris on the news?" Georgie asked.

"That would be good for us," said Saffron. "But it depends whether the Corporation is allowed to show it." She caught Viggo's eye and gave a quick nod towards the southern side of the square, where three police vans were pulling up. "Looks like the police have received their instructions from NJ7," she said to Georgie. "Time to go."

Viggo started to wrap up his speech. The parts that Georgie could pick up were about the dangers of having a government that didn't need to rely on the votes of the public. Some of the crowd were responding with cautious smiles and nods, while others looked confused – or even angry.

Suddenly, the whole square seemed to judder. There was a deep boom that echoed off the buildings and lingered in Georgie's ears. She staggered backwards and only just managed to keep her balance. The square became chaos. Screams pierced the traffic noise and there was the tinkle of hundreds of breaking windows. Several people had fallen over, but they were pushed away or trampled as the crowd scattered in all directions. When Georgie looked up she saw a pillar of smoke rising from beyond the rooftops. It was like a giant black reflection of the white stone of Nelson's Column, and just as unmissable.

Frozen in shock, she found herself running alongside her mother. In seconds they'd forced their way through the crowd to join the others. Felix and Saffron were helping Viggo protect his boxes of leaflets and his megaphone from the stampede.

"What's happening?" Georgie cried out.

"I don't know," Viggo called back calmly. "We need to get out of here and find a TV."

Jimmy drifted in and out of consciousness. He was vaguely aware of a screaming pain all over his body, but also the thrumming of his programming through his blood. It numbed the agony. It was keeping him alive.

Jimmy struggled to make sense of the flashes of the world that he saw around him. There were hundreds of people, sirens, blue lights, shouts. Then he realised he was moving – or being moved.

Somebody had wrapped a silver space-blanket round him and put him on a stretcher. Between moments of blackout, he saw the faces of other people – some of them children. A lot of them were also wrapped in space-blankets or on stretchers. Jimmy strained to remember how this had all happened. He wanted to ask somebody, but couldn't pull in the breath to speak. Was there something covering his mouth and nose? *Yes*, he realised slowly, *an oxygen mask.*

He blacked out again, but only for a few seconds. Now he found himself in the back of an ambulance. Who else was there with him? Paramedics? Other victims of the explosion? Jimmy's mind was overcome by questions. How could anybody have survived being in the tower block when it collapsed?

Gradually, Jimmy felt a little strength creeping back into his system. He felt like his body was in tatters, but sensed his programming churning inside him more fiercely than ever, healing him from within. Unfortunately he wasn't yet strong enough to stave off the next blackout. He gritted his teeth and tried to force his eyes to stay open, controlling his blinks as if they were one-handed press-ups. He failed.

When he came round again there were voices. Paramedics. They were radioing ahead to the hospital, describing the injured boy's condition. *They know nothing*, Jimmy thought. *They don't know who I am and they don't know all my injuries will heal faster than they've ever seen.*

Then he caught a snatch of the word "Tommy" on the ambulance radio and it finally sank in. The ambulance was rushing him to the very place he was desperate to be: St Thomas' Hospital. This was his chance to survive. His burns might heal themselves, but his radiation poisoning was another matter.

As the siren wailed, Jimmy's body tingled. He knew his whole body must be covered in terrible burns, but it was exhilarating to feel a prickle rising to the surface inside his scorched skin. His head was held in place by something, so he couldn't see what was happening to him, but he could feel the paramedics quickly covering almost every part of him with a cool dressing. He imagined his skin healing as they worked – a creeping redness covering the dull grey layer that he knew lay within.

The next thing Jimmy was conscious of was the ambulance tearing into the Accident and Emergency bay of the hospital. Jimmy forced what strength he had into his shoulders and arms to push himself on to his elbows. The paramedics rushed to push him back down, but Jimmy caught a glimpse of the hundreds of people pouring in to the hospital, some bleeding, some being carried, others wheeled on a stretcher like Jimmy. Most of them were covered in blood, but they were conscious and heading into the hospital. Jimmy was aghast at the injuries. Were all these people from the tower block?

The cries and the blood swirled around in his head, all illuminated by a single, powerful floodlight on top of a TV news van, even though it was still daylight. Then Jimmy saw the news reporter talking into a camera, her back to the chaos. It looked like the Corporation news van had arrived even before the ambulances. How was that possible?

Jimmy heard his own voice spinning through his skull like a distant echo. Then the oxygen mask was pressed over his face again and another tidal wave of darkness hit him.

07 LUCK OF THE EGYPTIAN

Eva Doren sat alone in Miss Bennett's office, waiting. Even though she was only thirteen, she'd become essential to the Head of NJ7 – personal assistant, secretary, even protégée. Her notepad and pen were ready in her hands for her usual note-taking job. But this time something felt different. First there was the urgency with which she'd been summoned, then there was the bustling in the NJ7 corridors. The atmosphere was more than simply busy. People seemed frightened. And this was the first time that Miss Bennett hadn't been in her office waiting for Eva to arrive.

Eva studied the walls. All of NJ7 Headquarters looked similar – grey concrete breeze blocks with the only colour provided by exposed electrical wiring. There were no windows – NJ7 was housed in a labyrinth of tunnels below Westminster.

Miss Bennett had obviously done her best to brighten up her part of the network. Postcards of old paintings of horses were stuck up on the walls and directly behind her desk there was a huge Union Jack flag. Like the one in the Cabinet briefing room, this also had an additional vertical green stripe in the centre.

But Eva wasn't looking at the decorations. She was trying to work out whether this room, like the rest of NJ7, was covered by security cameras. Elsewhere, the cameras were visible. In here, they were either hidden or there weren't any. And if there weren't any, then this was Eva's first chance to investigate some of Miss Bennett's secrets.

Of course, Eva already knew more than her fair share of secrets. After all, Miss Bennett took her almost everywhere. But that wasn't good enough for Eva. She stood up casually, as if she was just stretching her legs. She had to look for cameras without seeming suspicious, just in case. Her head was throbbing. Somewhere in that huge desk there might be plans concerning Jimmy Coates, or Jimmy's family, and what Miss Bennett planned to do to punish them for helping Jimmy to disappear. As Eva began her search, the discomfort spread down through her body until her stomach was churning. It made her sick just to imagine that she might find a document bearing the names of her friends – even her best friend, Georgie Coates.

She circled the desk, eyeing the drawers, unable to blink, and went back to her seat. The drawers were probably locked, but was it worth trying them? Eva realised she would never forgive herself if Jimmy or his family were harmed by NJ7 in an attack that she could have tried to warn them about. After all, that's why she was here. She lived with the constant fear that NJ7 would discover she was a traitor, working undercover for the Government's enemies. But that danger was worth it if she could find something that would really help Jimmy, or something that would end the rule of the current Government and replace it with a democracy. *Yes*, Eva thought, *I have to. This might be the only chance I ever get to be alone in this office.*

She stood up again. Her hands were shaking and she could barely keep a grip on her pencil. Her legs were suddenly stiff, but she forced them to move and stepped round the desk.

"Sorry to keep you waiting, Eva." Miss Bennett's voice stabbed into Eva's chest and stole the breath from her lungs. "I've been briefing some members of the press about the explosion." Eva didn't yet know about any explosion and Miss Bennett's words weren't sinking in. Her sudden arrival had frozen Eva to the spot. The Head of NJ7 strode in and took her seat behind her desk. Only now did Eva start to wonder what had exploded. She was about to find out.

"Take all of this down, Eva," Miss Bennett began. "You'll need to circulate a memo containing all these details…"

* * *

When Jimmy finally came to, he tried to work out how much time had passed. The sounds of the hospital had changed. Everything was much calmer, with no screaming, just the insistent whirring of the heating system and the distant clatter of a trolley in the corridor outside the ward.

Before he even realised he was doing it, his mind was running through his whole body, feeling the bandages and dressings, gently testing his joints and muscles. Only now did he notice the cool pressure from a gauze bandage that covered his whole head, except for a mouth hole and two holes for his eyes.

As his memories returned, Jimmy had to fight back panic. How many had survived the bomb? He tentatively manoeuvred himself until he was sitting up in bed. His pain was much less intense than earlier and he could tell that it wasn't just because his programming was numbing it. He must have actually gone some way towards healing as well. How long had he been in hospital?

The children's ward was packed. Extra beds had been squeezed in and all of them were occupied. The boy in the bed to Jimmy's left looked a little younger than him. He was sitting up as well, and Jimmy couldn't see immediately what injuries he'd suffered. Jimmy knew this was the perfect chance to gather some information, but he felt so awkward. It had been so long since he'd been in the company of people even remotely his own age. He felt completely out of place.

"Hey," he said, hearing the nervousness in his own voice. He had to remember how to speak and act like a normal human boy, not a genetically-created organic assassin.

The boy turned to look at him. Jimmy shuddered – the whole left half of the boy's head was swathed in a huge ball of bandage. He looked like he'd got his face stuck inside a giant ping-pong ball.

"Don't worry," the boy said with a smile. "Apparently it looks worse than it is. It doesn't really hurt. I'm going home in a couple of hours." Suddenly he realised something. "Oh, wait. Not home, but out of here anyway. Home's been blown up!"

Home, thought Jimmy. The word landed in his chest like a bomb. Everybody in that ward except him had a home, and even if it had been blown up, they'd find a new one. Jimmy felt a flash of longing to swap places with any of them.

"You from that tower block?" he asked, to force away his thoughts.

"Er, obviously," came the response. "Everybody here is. I thought you were too."

"Oh, yeah, sure." Jimmy told himself to blend in. He was already afraid the doctors would have noticed something unusual about him when they were treating him. The last thing he wanted was the other patients being suspicious of him as well. "I'm Michael," he lied, instinctively hiding his identity.

"Hi, Michael," the boy replied. "I'm Iqbar." He laughed nervously. "That must hurt a lot."

Jimmy's hands jumped to his face, but both were completely covered in bandage. He'd forgotten that he was wrapped up like an Egyptian mummy, but it made Jimmy less nervous about asking questions. After all, there was no way he could be recognised.

"No," Jimmy replied. "It doesn't hurt much. You know – looks worse than it is." He nodded casually and tried to smile, but wasn't sure whether that was even visible. "So er..." he hesitated, unsure how to ask the question on his mind. "How did, I mean... Are the people in this ward the only people who survived?"

Iqbar furrowed his brow in confusion. "Everybody survived except the car park attendant," he said, as if it was the most natural thing in the world. "There was nobody else in the block when it went down." Jimmy didn't think he could possibly have heard correctly. Maybe the bandages covering his ears were distorting things, but then Iqbar continued. "We all got out. Somebody set off the fire alarm and we thought it was, like, a fire drill. But it wasn't. Obviously."

The fire alarm? Jimmy's mind was racing. Could he possibly have saved everybody after all? He didn't dare think it could be true. He vaguely remembered smashing his hand against the fire alarm, but he hadn't heard it go off. He'd assumed the bombers had disabled it, but perhaps they hadn't. Could Jimmy have been that lucky?

No, he told himself, *not lucky.* It was the power inside him made him hit the fire alarm, and that's what had saved everybody. Not for the first time, Jimmy felt that strange mix of relief and fear. But he still didn't understand what was going on, or how there'd been enough time for everybody to evacuate before the bomb went off.

"What about all those people who were brought in at the same time as me...?" he said.

"Yeah," Iqbar replied matter-of-factly. "There were loads of people. It's from when half the building came down. There was, like, glass and rocks coming down on us, and a lot of people got burned a bit." He leaned towards Jimmy and dramatically pointed to his bandage. "I nearly lost an eye," he exclaimed. "Think what would have happened if the whole building had come down. Apparently it was just luck that the bomb wasn't in the middle of the car park, it was at stuck at the entrance, so it didn't do so much damage."

Luck again, Jimmy thought to himself, his insides fizzing.

"We were all standing there just watching it come down," Iqbar went on. "And I told everyone it was stupid to be standing so close, but they didn't believe me." He shrugged. "Anyway. You know. That's how it is."

"Yeah, I know how it is." Jimmy's voice was nonchalant, but inside he was flooded with relief. He'd done it. Without even knowing that it would have any effect, he'd set off the fire alarm and moved the bomb to the place in the car park where it would do the least damage. *I saved them,*

Jimmy thought, unable to believe it. *I saved everybody.* It was the first time he remembered that anything positive had come from his assassin programming. His joy was only dampened when he remembered that the men who'd loaded the bomb into the van, and the man who'd driven it into position, were still out there. And Jimmy had no idea who they were.

"Who put the bomb there?" Jimmy asked quietly. Iqbar looked at him like he was from another planet.

"Who d'you think?" he asked sarcastically. "It was the Frenchies."

"The French?" Jimmy gasped.

"Yeah. Everybody knows. We knew it straightaway."

"What about the metal shutter on the car park?" Jimmy asked. "Has that always been there?"

"No, those builders put that in this afternoon. Didn't you see them? They're the ones who filled up the stairwell with, like, rocks and stuff." Iqbar shook his head slowly. "I should have known it was the French then."

Jimmy was struggling to make sense of it all. Would France really try to blow up ordinary members of the public? And how had they managed to organise that kind of attack without British security forces having any idea it was happening?

Then his heart began pounding, as if it was trying to break out from underneath the layers of bandage. Everything had spiralled out of control. What if the British were planning to strike back? When they'd thought the French had blown up a British oil rig, they'd retaliated by attacking a French uranium mine. Jimmy imagined that any second there could be a British van driving explosives into the basement of a tower block in Paris. It had to stop. There was no reason for it.

I have to get out of here, he thought. He knew that the attack on the tower block was just a part of the ongoing battle between Britain and France – with Jimmy himself stuck in the middle. He hoped desperately that somebody out there was spreading his message about the oil rig, despite this new violence from the French.

Jimmy flexed his arms, then felt confident enough to pull out the wires that connected him to the machine next to the bed and swing his legs sideways to stand up.

"Hey," protested Iqbar. "What are you doing?"

"Thanks for the chat, Iqbar," Jimmy replied, watching the nurses at the end of the ward, trying to work out the rhythm of their conversation so he could move without being seen. "I hope your eye is OK."

"Are you going to the vending machine?" asked Iqbar. Jimmy didn't reply. "Will you get me some crisps?"

Jimmy shut out Iqbar's voice. He didn't want to be reminded of Felix, his best friend – or the fact that he was hungry. *Concentrate*, he told himself. *Do what you're here to do*. He had to forget about the temporary trouble his body was in – the burns and the bruises. He gathered his strength and prepared himself to find somebody – anybody – that knew about radiation poisoning. The trouble was, he had no idea how to do that.

He slipped out of the ward with ease, but out in the corridor he realised his injuries hadn't healed as much as he'd thought. Every shift in his body weight sent a stab of pain through his nerves. As if that wasn't bad enough, his whole body was covered in tight bandages, making it impossible to move easily or inconspicuously.

He walked as quickly as he could, but people passed him constantly. He had to slow to a shuffle and drop his head, hoping desperately that hospital staff would be too busy to concern themselves with why a patient in an obviously serious condition was out of bed.

He wasn't so lucky. The very first nurse that passed gave him a confused look. The next one did the same, and slowed down to watch him pass. Jimmy knew he didn't have long. He frantically rubbed away at his bandages as he went, loosening his hands and trying to unwrap himself. If he could reach the end of the corridor without being stopped, he could change his appearance in the lift, make it to another floor then look for some kind of information board that would give him a clue about where he should be going.

Then he heard the rapid tapping of footsteps behind him. When he picked up his pace, so did they. He could feel his programming surging to the forefront of his mind. It was building a picture of the person catching up with him – male, about 180 centimetres, slim build... It was also estimating the optimum moment to strike out and render this person unconscious.

Jimmy pushed on, extending his stride, hurrying without looking like he was hurrying. The rhythm of footsteps picked up speed. Jimmy could feel them hammering into his spine, every one closer and closer. If he could just reach the end of the corridor...

Jimmy heard the man's breathing close behind him. He didn't dare look back. He was terrified that if he did, he'd lose control and flatten this person before he could draw another breath. Instead he shuffled on. But then Jimmy himself felt flattened – by the man's calm, deep voice.

"Hello, Jimmy Coates. We need to have a little talk."

08 DOCTOR'S ORDERS

Jimmy slowly turned to look at the man looming over him. The rest of the corridor was suddenly deserted, as if the two of them were all alone in the world.

"How do you know who I am?" Jimmy asked quietly.

"I didn't until you just confirmed it. But it was worth an educated guess."

Jimmy was puzzled for a moment, but then his eyes jumped to the brown file in the man's hand. Suddenly it was obvious – this was a senior doctor who'd looked over the chart of Jimmy's progress since coming into the hospital. It must have made interesting reading.

The doctor reached out slowly. Very gently he unravelled the bandaging from around Jimmy's head. It took all of Jimmy's effort to let him. His programming fizzed, snarling at every touch. At last the boy's face was revealed. The doctor studied him intensely, biting his bottom lip. His eyes twinkled in a face that looked like padded leather – too tanned, too many creases.

His hair was dark grey and neatly trimmed.

"I heard rumours," he muttered, half to himself. "I followed some of the research in the journals all those years ago. It was fascinating. Then all mention of it suddenly disappeared and I remember wondering what happened. Lots of us did. That was so long ago. But when I saw the Government blaming some boy for an assassination... for chaos... I wondered... I didn't actually believe..."

Jimmy held himself completely still. His programming was ticking over, restless, itching to flatten this man and escape.

The doctor shook his head in awe. "At first I assumed this was full of mistakes." He gestured to his file. "You know – human error." His expression darkened. "Until I considered the possibility of superhuman recovery."

"There's always that possibility," said Jimmy softly. He could only imagine what his own face looked like now. It felt hot and cold all at once – uncomfortable, like he was wearing a skin that didn't fit him, but not too painful.

"Doctor," said Jimmy, interrupting the man's examination, "when they brought me in..." he paused, waiting for the doctor's full attention, "did they test for radiation poisoning?" The doctor's face froze.

"I think I'm ready for that little talk now," Jimmy added.

* * *

Up on the top floor of the hospital, Jimmy and the doctor rushed into an empty ward."This is the most isolated space we have," the doctor panted. "It's meant to be closed." He pointed to one corner, where a pile of cloths, buckets, a mop and some plumber's tools told half the story. The smell gave away the rest.

"It's just a precaution," the doctor went on, sounding panicky, "in case you still have traces of radioactive substances in your system."

"I haven't," Jimmy reassured him, wishing he could be more certain himself.

"OK, that's good. That would mean you can't harm anybody else, but we should take a blood test just in case." Growing ever more frantic, the doctor rushed to a bedside unit and scrabbled with the packaging of a syringe, then took a sample of his own blood. Jimmy was amazed that even a man with so much experience was shaking while he did it.

"Do you feel nauseous?" the man asked. Jimmy shook his head. "Have you been vomiting?"

"I haven't eaten anything," Jimmy replied, shaking his head again. "Do you have any crisps or something?"

The doctor ignored him, caught up in his thoughts, then babbled almost to himself, "If you had radiation sickness, you'd be vomiting, you'd be nauseous, your hair would be falling out... you might even be bleeding inside your mouth. It depends on the level of exposure. Are you more tired than normal?"

Jimmy shrugged. *Normal*. The word repeated in his head like a mocking laugh. He couldn't stop it.

"Never mind," said the doctor. "We won't know for sure until we've tested anyway. Come on!" He flapped urgently towards the same bedside unit. "I'm not coming any closer than I have to, so you can take blood yourself."

Jimmy was taken aback, but tugged at his bandaging to free his hands and expose his forearm so he could draw a blood sample. He grimaced when he saw his skin. It was marbled with red and grey. It was like a battleground where the explosion had flayed his flesh and his body was fighting back. Jimmy forced himself to look away from his burns. He calmly unpacked another syringe and without hesitation he jabbed it into his arm.

"If you've heard the rumours about who... about what I am," said Jimmy, trying to sound relaxed to put the doctor at ease, "then maybe you've also heard the truth about Britain and France going to war."

"The truth?" the doctor scoffed. "That might be *your* truth, boy, but the rest of this country knows full well that the French are a threat and this Government is doing its best to defend the nation. You spreading lies just puts every true British citizen in danger. Look at what happened today! You witnessed the French blowing up a London tower block! Still think we can all be friends?"

Jimmy rolled the syringe of his blood across the floor. Maybe the doctor was right. Maybe today's explosion just proved Jimmy had been wrong all along. It didn't matter who was to blame for what – the two nations were destined to go to war and nobody could stop them until they'd destroyed each other. They had that power.

"I don't believe it," Jimmy said suddenly, as if replying to his own thoughts. Even if the whole of the British Government was crazy, and the whole of the French Government was crazy too, Jimmy refused to believe that there weren't enough sane people in both countries to stop a war. But unlike the Governments, the only power the people had was the truth – and Jimmy was the person who could deliver it to them.

The doctor snatched up the syringe and cupped it in his hand, staring at the blood.

"I'm going to find some pretty amazing things in here, aren't I?" he said, his eyes wide. Then he glanced nervously at Jimmy. "I need to take this to the lab, but..."

"It's OK," said Jimmy. "I promise I won't go anywhere. I'll wait here."

The doctor's relief was obvious. On his way out he pulled a dust sheet off a TV trolley and turned on the set. "They control the channel at reception, I'm afraid," he declared as he left.

Jimmy didn't feel in the mood to watch TV, but the screen very quickly drew him in. He couldn't remember the last time he'd had the chance to watch anything. It felt like a connection to his old life – even though it was the Corporation rolling news channel, which he would never have dreamed of watching before, and there was no sound.

They were showing pictures of the collapsed tower block. Half the building was still standing, with people's kitchens and bedrooms ripped down the middle, as if Godzilla had chewed up the rest. Jimmy was fascinated. It was so strange seeing what it looked like from the outside, and after everything had happened. Nothing could capture the heat or the noise, or the light that seemed to burst through Jimmy's head when he thought about it.

Then the image switched to the scenes of the casualties being brought in to the hospital. It took a few seconds for Jimmy to connect the pictures on the screen with the fact that he'd lived through this. One of those ambulances was the one that had brought him to where he was sitting now. His memories of it were hazy pictures flashing through his mind in total disorder. He had to shut his eyes for a moment to set things straight.

When he opened them the news had moved on to the next item. There was an incredibly tall Asian man addressing a press conference. The caption rolled across the bottom of the screen: PM IAN COATES COLLAPSES, RUSHED TO HOSPITAL. WILLIAM LEE CALLS FOR CALM.

Jimmy's chest lurched. He stared at the words repeating on the TV as if they'd have a new meaning the second, third or fourth time. He looked for the volume control on the TV, but there wasn't one. He assumed that was also controlled from some central system. He blinked rapidly, as if what he was seeing was irritating his eyes. What had happened to Ian Coates? Was this William Lee in charge now? Who was he? Jimmy had never heard of him.

He forced himself to stare at William Lee's mouth, trying to lip-read, but the camera cut away too often for him to make sense of anything. In any case, that wasn't the real reason Jimmy was concentrating on Lee. He was desperate to distract himself from the swirling in his gut and fizz in his sinuses. *He's not my real father*, Jimmy reminded himself, forcing back the emotion. But he was losing the fight. He hated himself for acting as if he still cared about the health of Ian Coates.

Zafi Sauvage sat cross-legged on her top bunk at the youth hostel while students and travellers wandered in and out of the dormitory.

"Aw, cute bunny," said a teenage girl, seeing a fluffy toy rabbit in Zafi's hands. She pointed to the rabbit's T-shirt and giggled. It had YOU'RE THE BEST printed on it in bright red letters. "What's his name?"

Zafi stared blankly at the girl and stabbed her penknife into the middle of the bunny's chest. The teenager backed away and rushed out of the room. Zafi couldn't help giggling. She carefully extended the slit down the centre of her new toy and opened up a cavity among the stuffing. The rabbit was perfect for the job – easy to handle, easy to conceal and about the size of a hand grenade. She was about to start the delicate process of arranging the explosives inside it when her phone vibrated. It had to be her contact at the DGSE. *Can't they just trust me and let me get on with it?* she thought to herself. At the same time she knew they were right to be checking up on her, after her failure on the last mission.

She checked the message, and sure enough it was another encrypted text from the French Secret Service. But as her mind spun the letters and numbers into new shapes to decrypt their meaning, Zafi's confusion grew. Her bosses were congratulating her. "Good job," said the message. "Is the mission complete?"

Zafi had to read it several times, just to make sure she'd decoded it properly. *The mission hasn't even started yet*, she said to herself, bemused. Her fingers were already tapping through the functions on her phone, accessing the Corporation news feed. And that's when she discovered her mission had just become a little more complicated: Ian Coates had collapsed – and it had nothing to do with her.

Jimmy was startled by the click of the door. The doctor strode in and Jimmy turned away to wipe his eyes.

He regretted it when he felt how raw his skin was.

"What's all this about?" he asked boldly, still not making eye contact.

"You mean that?" the doctor replied, waving at the TV. "You didn't hear about the Prime Minister? He collapsed."

"I can see that," Jimmy muttered through clenched teeth. "I've been doing all my own reading for a while now. What's wrong with him?"

The doctor huffed and was about to say something when the news moved on to the next item. Jimmy caught it in the corner of his eye and whipped his head round to watch it so fast his neck gave a loud click.

"Turn the sound up!" Jimmy begged, rushing up to the screen.

"I can't. It's—"

"But..." Jimmy fumbled round the edges of the set again, vainly hoping he'd overlooked the volume control the first time. "I have to hear this!" Finally he had to give up and gripped the sides of the TV, watching intently.

"What's the matter?" asked the doctor. Jimmy could hardly hear him. On the screen was footage of some kind of public demonstration in Trafalgar Square. It was hard to tell how many people were there – Jimmy thought that perhaps they were deliberately choosing camera angles that didn't show the crowd – but the upturned plastic box at the centre was clear. From there, a tall man with shoulder-length, dark blond hair was addressing the square through a megaphone – Christopher Viggo.

Viggo was the man the British Government had most to fear from. An ex-NJ7 agent and a fanatical opponent of Neo-democracy, he was a constant thorn in their side, travelling the country in secret, gathering support wherever he could. The Government wanted him dead – and once they'd even sent Jimmy to do the job. That was supposed to have been Jimmy's first mission, but he'd rebelled against it at the last moment. Ever since, Jimmy had also been on NJ7's hit list, and Viggo had strived to convince more and more people that Neo-democracy was an evil abuse of power.

In these images, Viggo was speaking as passionately as ever, with his full-length navy coat flapping in the breeze like a cape. But Jimmy wasn't watching Viggo. He wasn't even thinking about what the man might be saying. Because in the very corner of the screen, standing by the makeshift stage and drifting in and out of the shot, was Helen Coates. Jimmy's mother.

"When was this?" Jimmy gasped, unable to tear his eyes away from the images. Then he shouted, "When did this happen?"

"That was this morning," the doctor replied, taken aback. "And you're not missing anything with the sound down – they always blank out his voice and have an actor reading some of the things he said. And I can tell you..." He punctuated his sentence with a soft chortle, awkwardly trying to ease the tension. "...the things that man says go from dangerous to hilarious to just plain crazy!"

"She's alive," Jimmy whispered, letting the doctor's words fade into the background. "She's with Chris. They must all be alive." He was thinking rapidly now, trying to work out if there was any reason why Felix and Georgie wouldn't be with his mother and Viggo. "They're alive. They're OK."

This time, Jimmy didn't want to fight the emotion. It felt wonderful – as if he was coming alive again after being a zombie. Happiness suffused his whole body. His smile stretched his lips almost to his ears. It tested the burns on his face that were far from healed, but he didn't care about the pain. It was washed away by the tears rolling down his cheeks.

Jimmy held his head for a second, then jumped up. "Yes!" he shouted. "They're alive!" He turned to the doctor. "I have to go and find them! Will you get ready to treat me when I come back? I'll... I dunno... make an appointment or something."

The doctor looked confused and a little bit scared. "Hold on, Jimmy," he insisted. "You think I can let you go running around London like a wild animal?"

"But you said yourself if I don't have radioactive stuff actually on me, then I'm not contagious, so I—"

"It's ridiculous, Jimmy." The doctor threw up his hands in exasperation. "You're sick."

"I don't feel sick," Jimmy protested.

The doctor raised his hands to the ceiling, then clapped them together as if pleading with the ceiling fan.

"Listen to me," he ordered. "Wait here until the sample comes back from the lab."

Jimmy was about to protest, but the words stopped on his tongue. Had the doctor said "sample" or "*samples*"? How many samples had the man sent to the lab? One or two? Jimmy's elation froze. He wasn't sure what was going on, but suspicion dug into his brain. He decided to try a little test.

"Thank you for helping me, doctor," he said softly, playing the innocent child.

The doctor eyed Jimmy warily. "It's my duty," he replied. "As a doctor."

"But it's so brave," Jimmy went on, pushing as far as he could go. "And it must have been a hard decision to make – do you treat me, or do you protect your career, your hospital... possibly even your own life? So, seriously..." He paused and dropped his voice to an emphatic whisper. "...Thank you."

"*Thank* you!?" the doctor spluttered suddenly. "Did you think I was going to *treat* you?!"

Jimmy squirmed as if he'd picked up a bad smell. He was disgusted at how easily the doctor's act had crumbled.

"I couldn't treat you even if I wanted to!" the doctor went on, throwing his head back in derision. "All I can do is send the blood to the lab. It's not personal, Jimmy. Even if it turns out *I'm* infected already, I can't help myself. I've put in a call to Professor Wilson at the

Hollingdale Institute. Zigmund is the only one who could possibly do anything about it!" His chest juddered with a silent laugh. "You thought I was going to *treat* you? An enemy of the State? I'd be thrown in prison for the rest of my life! I was only talking to you until..." He marched towards the door.

"Until what?" Jimmy called out, but the man didn't stop. *Run him down*, Jimmy heard himself growling inside. *Stop him. End him.* He felt his muscles go rock solid, set for violence. *No*, Jimmy ordered himself. "Please," he begged, forcing his words out against his own body's will. "I need you!"

The doctor paused at the door. He turned round, but his eyes swept the floor. He couldn't look at Jimmy. "It's too late, Jimmy," he announced, a new tremor in his voice.

"No, it isn't," Jimmy protested. "You can still—"

"You don't understand. The building's in lockdown..." He trailed off and stared out of the window.

"What are you saying?" Jimmy asked, but the question didn't seem to register on the doctor's face. "If you can't help me, put me back in the ward. Forget about me. Let me be..."

"What?" the doctor snapped. "Normal? But you..." His voice faded away, then he muttered, more to himself, "When you cried..." He squinted at Jimmy, as if he'd seen something new in him. The doctor opened his mouth, but didn't seem able to find the right words. "If I'd known, Jimmy, I would never have..." He gulped and opened the door. "I was just following my instructions. I was to keep you occupied until extra security could... Sorry," he whispered finally. "I can't help you now."

He rushed out and hurriedly slammed the door after him. Jimmy jumped to his feet to follow, but was stopped by a rumble in his stomach. The drawers of the bedside units started rattling. The clatter grew louder, then the beds themselves shifted on their wheels, vibrating with the floor.

Jimmy watched through the square window of reinforced glass in the door as the doctor locked the ward from the outside. Jimmy was still struggling to make sense of the man's words. Then he heard the drone of engines. He turned to look out of the window. Between the slats of the Venetian blinds he could see the silhouettes of a fleet of helicopters – the same helicopters that had chased him from Hailsham. They charged towards the hospital, keeping perfect formation and maintaining their altitude at precisely the level of the top floor – where Jimmy was standing, alone.

A second later, they opened fire.

09 THE OTHER WING

Jimmy dived to the floor. All around him the windows shattered and bullets pinged against the lino. The TV screen became a smoking pile of sparks and splintered plastic. The choppers were strafing the entire floor with machine gun fire.

Jimmy crawled under one of the beds. He could see the exit, but there was no way he could make a dash for it. Between him and the door was a hailstorm of bullets. He wanted to curl up under the bed and close his eyes, but he could already feel that the dark power in his blood had other ideas. It gripped his brain, squeezing out the fear.

In a flash, Jimmy scampered across the floor, holding the bed frame over his head and wheeling it above him like his own giant tortoise shell. When he reached the next bed, he moved under it, and used that as his shield instead. He rushed from bed to bed, butting each one up against the next to create an unbroken protective roof.

He could hear the shots ripping into the mattresses above him. Some bullets even tore straight through and lodged in the thin metal springs, barely millimetres from the top of Jimmy's head.

At the end of the room he calculated whether he could break through the locked door with one ram. But then he peered out from under the bed and his thinking changed in an instant. There was a shadow across the window in the door. Then someone crossed in front of it – a figure in black.

Jimmy winced. *There has to be another way out*, he thought. He wheeled towards the pile of mops, buckets and rags in the corner of the room. They'd been shot to pieces, but Jimmy was able to salvage a short length of mop handle. He tested the wood, trying to work out whether it would hold his weight.

What am I doing? he thought desperately as his hands worked. He seemed to be constantly a step behind his own brain, conscious of only snippets of the plan. When he pieced them together he was horrified. *Can I do this?* At the same time he knew he had no choice. The only other way out of this room was through the window.

Jimmy tested the broken mop handle against the legs of the bed, making sure that it wouldn't pass between them horizontally. It was just long enough. He positioned two buckets underneath it to stop it twisting and slipping under the bed frame, then turned his attention to his bandaging.

His whole body was still encased in white gauze bandage. It flapped around his hands where he'd wriggled them free and was loose on one arm as well, from when he'd taken the blood sample. But the rest of him was tightly wrapped. It looked like a single length of bandage running dozens of times round his torso, then down his right leg and back up again to go down the other leg, and end at his left ankle. At least, Jimmy hoped it was a single, unbroken bandage. If it wasn't, his plan was going to end with a cruel splat.

Still the bullets hammered around him. He had to shut it all out. The slightest miscalculation now would have consequences as serious as any bullet. He pulled on the end of the bandage that hung round his arm and tested it with three sharp tugs. It seemed strong enough, but strength wasn't all Jimmy needed. He had to have elasticity.

Jimmy had never bungee jumped before, but he'd heard enough about it to understand the principle – a free dive from a great height with strong elastic attached to your ankles, which pulled you up again just a fraction before you hit the ground. It could be the perfect escape. There were, however, a few snags: he was using bandage instead of elastic. He didn't know how long the bandage around him would be when it all unravelled. And he had no idea how tall the building was. *Apart from that*, he thought with a deep breath, *it's a perfect plan*.

He glanced up at the window, where the Venetian blind was dancing under the barrage of bullets. He knew he was on the top floor, but how high up was that? He could take a guess, but a guess wasn't good enough. He could feel his mind whirring, recalling every piece of information it had, but the only time he'd seen the building from the outside was when he'd been barely conscious.

With a grunt of frustration he returned to his bandaging. He looked himself up and down, frantically trying to work out the length of the cloth wrapped around him. It seemed impossible – like guessing the number of sweets in a giant jar. Jimmy tried to think, but the bullets ripped through his concentration.

"Come on!" he shouted out loud. Any second the helicopters would make way for the Special Forces. *Don't bother measuring*, he told himself at last. As long as the length of the bandage, plus the length of Jimmy's body, came to less than the height of the building, he would survive. He tied one end of the bandage round the mop handle, then teased out the other end by loosening the bandaging round his left calf. When he'd found enough of the end he tied it tightly round his ankle.

He double-checked his knots, unable to force away the two terrifying images that haunted him. In one, the bandage snapped and Jimmy smashed head first into the hospital forecourt. In the other, Jimmy was left dangling where the helicopter gunmen could pick him off, like a worm on a fishing line.

Then came silence. The shooting had stopped. Jimmy's time was up. The click of the door shattered the protection of his hiding place. He peered out in time to see the first set of huge black boots pounding into the ward. Jimmy swallowed his fear with one huge gulp and burst out from under the bed with an explosion of power.

The Special Forces soldiers swivelled to shoot. All they saw of Jimmy was a streak of white crashing through the Venetian blind. Jimmy heard the gun fire, but it instantly faded, replaced by the breeze. Jimmy seemed to hang in the sky for a second, the fresh air awakening his hope. Maybe this crazy plan was possible. Maybe he was going to make it and his programming had saved him again. For a split-second he had the sensation that he could fly.

Then he started to drop. The velocity stole the breath from his lungs. It felt like his heart was going to punch through his throat and come out the top of his head. But that was just the first couple of metres – the easy part. After that came the inevitable unravelling of Jimmy's bandaging.

The blue of the sky and grey of the street merged into one horrible mess. Jimmy spun round so fast it felt like his brain was twisting out of sync with his body – as if it wasn't just the bandage unravelling, but Jimmy's entire being as well. At first he tried to hold himself strong, but his roll was too rapid. His muscles went limp. His arms flailed about like useless wings and his head rocked back and forth until he thought it would snap off.

After a few seconds the rhythm of his spinning settled and he was able to distinguish which direction the ground was in. Unfortunately it was zooming towards him. Jimmy could feel his upper body was exposed to the cold now, then his weight shifted as the bandaging started reeling off his right leg. He keeled over in his fall until he was completely upside-down, spinning round his leg.

I was wrong, Jimmy thought. *There's too much bandage.* Suddenly the axis of his rotation changed again – the other leg was unwrapping itself. *There's still too much*, he thought. *I'm too close to the ground. I'm going to...*

Jimmy's terror was wrenched from his heart. The last metre of the bandage unspooled and he felt his ankle bearing the huge pressure. If it had been an ordinary rope, his foot would have been pulled clean off his leg, but there was enough elasticity in the bandage to slow him down more gradually. He kept spinning with the momentum of the unravelling gauze, and he could feel the blood pooling in his head. He knew he was slowing down, even though the pavement still surged towards him. He was travelling fast enough for his whole skull to smash into smithereens on impact.

Jimmy closed his eyes, tensed his body and wrapped his arms around his head, desperately hoping his bones were strong enough to stay intact. But the impact didn't come. Jimmy winced. He felt his whole skeleton screaming as the joints were pulled to breaking point, then the tips of the hairs on his head brushed gently against the ground. The bandage was at full stretch. It was as if he'd jumped with a perfectly calibrated bungee cord.

He hung there for what seemed like eons, waiting for the inevitable spring upwards. With a flood of wonderful disbelief, Jimmy felt the rush of the wind return and opened his eyes. With so much blood surging around his optic nerves he could hardly focus.

Jimmy felt lighter than air again as he was thrown up, tumbling over himself. His skin prickled at the cold – without the covering of the bandage he was left in just hospital underpants, but that was far from his biggest problem.

He levelled out about a third of the way up the building, and that's when he finally pulled his body under control. He transferred his weight with the slightest twitch of his muscles. They responded before he even knew what he was trying to do. The views of the streets and the shouts of the people below him were pushed into the background by the commanding, rapid-fire decision of the system inside him.

He felt his back arching, his arms stretching out to the side. He was poised in an elegant dive, controlling his descent expertly. Then he realised that his programming had no intention of heading for the ground a second time. There were too many people down there. Instead, Jimmy swung himself towards the building. His trepidation melted into exhilaration. He had dived from the top floor of the building and survived. Not only that, but he was now in complete control.

Now Jimmy was calm enough to notice more details of what was happening around him. Inevitably, a crowd had gathered to watch. People were being marshalled out of the way by security agents. If Jimmy reached the ground, there would be Special Forces waiting for him. Mid-flight, he glanced up. He just caught a glimpse of a line of heads sticking out of the top-floor windows – and the line of guns that came with them.

Just as Jimmy was about to hit the side of the building, he jerked his head backwards, leading his body into a backwards somersault. He couldn't stay still for a moment. If he did, he was sure he'd be shot down. *Don't they even care that they'd be shooting a child in full view of the public?* Jimmy wondered.

After a double roll, Jimmy caught the bandage and scurried upwards, hand over hand, swinging back towards the building. How long before the soldiers in the building cut the bandage? He hit the wall at the third floor, but was more than ready. He thrust his legs forwards and pushed himself off the wall with his bare feet. He heard the crack of guns. The bullets pinged into the brickwork of the hospital. Dust spattered his face, but Jimmy was already away.

He swung round the corner of the building, which took him over a security wall. It was perfect – nobody from the forecourt could follow him unless they came through the hospital itself and out of the side exit. This time when his feet made contact with the building, his legs were pumping at full pace. The impetus of his swing carried him on for a few precious moments, sprinting up the wall. Then, just as the bandage reached full stretch, Jimmy dug his fingers into tiny indents in the brickwork.

He strained to hold himself in place, but he knew he had to move before the gunmen found him and took aim. He clung on with one hand while with the other he reached down and undid the knot at his ankle. Then he kicked against the wall and flipped backwards, aiming for the top of a tree. He landed in the upper branches with an awkward crunch of bone on wood. *Softer than a hospital mattress*, Jimmy thought, spitting a leaf out of his mouth.

The burns all over Jimmy's body screamed for attention. Every branch of the tree seemed to stab or scratch at his skin as he clambered down to the ground. But he wasn't in the street. He realised that when he'd flown over the security wall he hadn't escaped the hospital complex, he'd leapt back into it.

St Thomas' Hospital was made up of two huge buildings immediately next door to each other. One was the block for the public hospital – that's the one Jimmy had been in. But now he found himself in the car park of the other part of the facility – the private wing.

With relief, he spotted a ramp that led down to the lower level of the car park, and when he made it to the bottom of the ramp he could see an exit to the street. Jimmy assumed NJ7 agents were already on their way between the wings of the hospital to find him. He had to keep moving, stay out of CCTV range and change his appearance as quickly as possible. *Clothes would help*, he thought, shivering in his scratchy hospital pants.

His limbs seemed to already have the solution. Jimmy found himself stalking through the car park along the line of vehicles. He hunched down to look through the drivers' windows. At the other end of the line, by a service door into the hospital, two figures were sitting in their car. Jimmy was already working out how best to fit into adult sized clothes.

Still three cars away from his target, Jimmy dropped to the ground and rolled underneath the adjacent vehicles. He sprang up next to the driver's door and pulled it open with one fluid movement.

"Take off your shirt and trousers now!" he ordered in a low, stern voice. It didn't have the effect he was expecting.

The driver was a huge black man – not fat, but even sitting at the wheel it was obvious he was over 185 centimetres tall and his chest was like a concrete bunker. He looked at Jimmy slowly, munching on the last crisp in a packet. His expression was completely blank, except for a hostile stare.

"I don't think this shirt will fit you, son," he said in a

110

deep murmur, crumpling the empty packet in his fist. Jimmy looked down at the shirt stretched across the man's awesome pecs. It bore a small, subtle logo: a green stripe.

"And I don't think mine is quite your style," added the man in the passenger seat, keeping his eyes straight ahead. He was also in a black shirt with the green stripe on his chest catching the light.

Only now did the second man glance at Jimmy. His eyes widened. "Hey," he gasped. "You're that boy... You're—"

Before another sound could escape the man's mouth, Jimmy was in action. He jumped up, aiming both his knees at the driver's face. In the same movement he leaned over the roof, flipped forwards on to his back and landed with his heels on the other side of the car, flying into the top of the other man's head as he emerged from the passenger door.

They were strong men, but the sudden attack caught them off guard. *Weren't they expecting me?* Jimmy wondered. *Why didn't they have their weapons already drawn?* He'd never known NJ7 agents to be so unprepared.

Jimmy dragged their unconscious bodies out of the car one at a time and lay them on the tarmac. Why hadn't they recognised him immediately? The only explanation was that they were here on some other mission. But what other assignment could two NJ7 agents be on that required them to be at this hospital?

Jimmy quickly pulled the shirt and trousers off the smaller agent. The man wasn't much smaller than his partner though. Jimmy had to roll up the sleeves of the shirt, turn up the trouser legs and pull the belt so tight around his middle that he needed to force a new hole in the leather to fasten the buckle. He took a pair of socks as well, but decided the oversized shoes would only slow him down.

He knew he had a matter of seconds before these agents came to or somebody spotted the disturbance. He glanced round the interior of the car and snatched a London street map from the floor. One destination was drumming through his head – the Hollingdale Institute. He even had a name: Professor Zigmund Wilson. If that's where a senior doctor at this hospital would go with radiation poisoning, then that's where Jimmy had to get to. If only he knew where it was.

He couldn't stop himself glancing at his fingers again. His skin was so raw they were almost glowing red. *That will heal*, Jimmy told himself. It felt as if his skin was soothing itself with every second that passed. It was the blueness on his fingertips Jimmy wasn't so sure about. It had spread even in the short time since he'd last looked at it. His toes had looked the same. He tried to work out whether he felt nauseous or wanted to vomit, but couldn't separate real symptoms from psychological ones. How damaged was his body?

And was the damage spreading or being healed?

He didn't know what address to look for to find the Hollingdale Institute, but he quickly realised that didn't matter – attached to the NJ7 agent's belt was a mobile phone. That was all he needed.

Jimmy dashed out of the car park, at last making it to the street. On the way, he checked one of the signs outside the hospital and punched the phone number into the agent's mobile. He ran on as he waited for somebody to pick up, and kept going while he spoke, not caring which direction he was heading, just glad to be putting some distance between himself and the hospital.

"Hello," he said, twisting his voice without intending to into the voice of an old man. "I have an appointment with Professor Wilson, but I didn't write down the time. Could you check it for me, please?"

"Professor Wilson?" said the receptionist.

"Yes, that's right. Professor Zigmund Wilson."

"There's no Zigmund Wilson at this hospital."

"Oh, is this the Hollingdale Institute?"

"No, this is St Thomas' Hospital."

"I'm sorry," said Jimmy, a smile breaking out on his face. "I must have the wrong number. Do you know how I can reach the Hollingdale Institute?"

"I have the number here, hold on one moment."

Jimmy slipped into the mouth of an alley between two boarded-up shops and peered back round the corner to check the street. He was constantly aware of the threat of being tracked, and every second that this phone was in his hand he was even more vulnerable. At last the receptionist came back on the line and gave Jimmy a number.

"And that's in Hackney, isn't it?" Jimmy said, as if it was the most natural thing in the world.

"No, no, that's wrong," replied the receptionist. "The Hollingdale Institute is in Mill Hill. It says here that it's on the Ridgeway, Mill Hill."

Jimmy snapped the phone shut, slipped it down a drain and ran north.

"Will he survive?" barked William Lee, marching through the corridors of the NJ7 bunkers with a mobile phone pressed against his ear. "Answer my question, doctor!" he shouted. "Will he survive?!"

He reached a small metal door marked discreetly with the number 10 and charged straight through it. Suddenly the bare concrete walls and strip lights gave way to a different world: thick carpet, lavish interiors, walls lined with old paintings of grim-faced politicians.

When Lee reached the Prime Minister's study he snapped the phone shut without saying goodbye. The room was packed with people, who all turned to give him their full attention. Some were the same people who'd been gathered round the Cabinet table when

Ian Coates collapsed, others were senior detectives, civil servants and Secret Service staff.

"Listen very carefully," Lee announced. "The doctors have ruled out heart failure. They've ruled out a stroke. They've ruled out aneurism and a dozen other conditions that sounded like gibberish to me." He cast his eye across the faces in front of him. After what he'd just heard from the doctor at the hospital, he couldn't shake the feeling that somebody in the room had attempted murder.

"It's their informed opinion," Lee went on, dropping his voice, "that the Prime Minister collapsed because of unnatural toxins." There was a moment's silence as the news sunk in. "Poison." A harrowed murmur broke out around the room. "Detective!" A bearded man in a brown suit stepped forward.

"Yes, sir?"

"I'm assigning an NJ7 research lab for your forensic team so that no evidence needs to leave this site, understand?" The man nodded. "Take everything down into the bunkers," Lee ordered. "Analyse every scrap and every particle of dust."

He gestured to everybody standing around him. "The doctors can't cure the PM until they know what poison is killing him. The chances are high that there are still traces of it in this room. Find it. The Prime Minister's life is in our hands."

He pulled out his phone to make another call, but

barked one final thought before leaving: "After his collapse and the bombing today, he's become the most popular British Prime Minister this century. The public is behind him. So good luck."

10 THE HOLLINGDALE INCIDENT

The Ridgeway in Mill Hill was a long, winding road which looked as if it belonged in the country, not the suburbs of London. On either side were high banks of trees casting deep shadows. In the fading daylight Jimmy was hardly visible to the drivers of the few cars that whizzed past.

He pushed his sleeves up again. The NJ7 shirt was starting to annoy him, but it was the only one he had. What's more, he knew the fabric was state-of-the-art. It was keeping him warm in a biting wind and was probably even soothing his burns, which were hardly uncomfortable any more. Still, he'd have gladly swapped the shirt for a jumper and a pair of shoes.

It had taken him longer than he'd expected to walk here, but he knew that it was safest to travel on foot for now. When NJ7 lost him at the hospital they would have immediately extended the search to cover all buses, trains and cars passing through the vicinity. As it was,

Jimmy didn't understand why he hadn't already encountered a ring of Special Forces and police. Surely NJ7 would also have set up a perimeter patrol and stopped anybody walking away from the hospital?

Jimmy tried to shrug off his anxiety, but the closer he came to the Hollingdale Institute the more edgy he felt. *It's just paranoia*, he told himself.

At last he rounded a bend and saw his destination. This was no ordinary hospital facility. It looked more like Batman's country manor – a huge building, with turrets and towers of grey/blue stone that twisted into the clouds. Jimmy wouldn't have been surprised to see a bolt of lightning split the sky or a vampire stalking the rooftops.

He jogged to the main gate, keeping pace with one of the security cameras as it swivelled, staying just outside its field of vision. Every step was guided by a force inside him that locked his muscles in precise movements. The booth at the main gate was empty. Jimmy felt a prickle of suspicion, but he had to press on. If there was the chance that somebody here could help him, it was worth the risk of an ambush.

He ducked under the vehicle barrier and in seconds he'd reached the door of the main building. That too was unguarded. *This place is deserted*, Jimmy thought to himself. Would Professor Wilson even be here?

Jimmy stepped cautiously into the main reception area. It was an old Victorian hallway, with navy tiles and an ornate plasterwork ceiling. Jimmy's eyes darted up and down the corridors that stretched out on either side. They were dark except for a dim light coming from a doorway at one far end. He crept along the corridor, his footsteps as silent as the rest of the building. He felt a struggle stirring inside him. Breaching security shouldn't have been this easy. It felt like a trap.

No, Jimmy told himself, refusing to give in to his fears. He didn't have a choice. And if radiation poisoning was going to kill him anyway, what did he have to lose? Being ambushed now would only make things simpler. He grimaced with determination and strained against his programming, using the energy to propel himself forwards, step by step.

He swung round into the doorway, bracing himself for a counter-attack, but there was nobody in the room. Jimmy was looking into a small office, with the blinds drawn. Books lined the walls and there was an old desk in the centre of the room with a lamp on it that threw a pool of pale yellow light around the middle of the room. Jimmy felt like a fool. He told himself to return to the lobby so he could begin to track down Professor Wilson properly. But then a whisper shattered the silence.

"Jimmy!"

The voice stabbed into Jimmy's brain. Suddenly his blood was pumping at triple speed. He peered into the shadows in the corner of the room and watched a slim figure step into the lamplight.

"Eva!" Jimmy's mouth dropped open, then melted into a smile. As soon as he felt the tingle of joy at seeing his sister's best friend, it was snatched away by the expression on her face. With her eyes stretched wide and her lips pursed she was a picture of fear. Jimmy was about to run to her, but froze at the tiny, almost imperceptible shake of Eva's head. Then her eyes flitted around the room, first to the lamp, then to three points on the bookshelves.

Without moving his head, Jimmy followed her guidance and realised what he was meant to see – like fireflies pinned at different points around the room, four tiny lenses reflected the glow of the lamp. Jimmy and Eva were being watched.

"I've been waiting for you," Eva announced, her voice flat and deliberately empty of emotion. Jimmy knew he had to be careful. NJ7 must be watching and any sign that Eva and Jimmy were still on the same side would be a catastrophe. As far as they knew, Eva had betrayed Jimmy and was working against him.

"I didn't expect to see you again," Jimmy snarled. He saw Eva's face relax slightly now she knew Jimmy was going to maintain the illusion that they were enemies.

"I'm sorry about what happened, Jimmy," Eva protested, a glint in her eye. "I had to do it, believe me." Jimmy was impressed by her acting. It even looked like she was enjoying this a little. "But I want to help you now."

Jimmy didn't know how to answer. He felt a surge of hope. Eva had always been clever – perhaps she really had found a way of helping him right under the noses of NJ7.

"Your burns…" Eva whispered, reaching towards him.

"You can't help me," Jimmy replied, pushing her hand away. He had to force his words and his voice to send out the exact opposite of the emotion thumping in his chest. "How did you find me?"

"The doctor who helped you at the hospital," Eva explained, her words rushing out. "He wasn't meant to let you escape."

"I suppose Miss Bennett has punished him for that."

"Badly." The sudden note of desolation in Eva's voice seemed genuine. Jimmy couldn't bear to imagine what NJ7 had done to that doctor simply because their plan to ensnare Jimmy at the hospital had failed.

"He told us that this was the only place you could be going," Eva went on. "He said he'd accidentally mentioned the name of it and you might have remembered."

Jimmy nodded slowly, the implications filtering through his mind. It wasn't just the name of the institute that the doctor had mentioned… Eva seemed to read his mind.

"Professor Wilson…" She couldn't finish her sentence. Tears trembled in her eyes. Jimmy felt a horrible queasiness in his gut. He rushed forwards and pushed Eva out of the way. There, curled up on the floor behind the desk, was the body of a middle-aged man. His piercing blue eyes stared up at the ceiling. The muscles in his throat seemed tense, as if he'd died in the middle of a scream. His square-rimmed glasses were twisted across the bridge of his nose.

Jimmy shook with rage. "What did they...?" He swallowed his question and instead punched his fists against the desk. He cracked straight through the wood, then swept his palms across the table top, letting out a blood-curdling cry. Professor Wilson's papers flew all over the room. The lamp crashed to the ground, but didn't break, so its light shone straight up into Jimmy's face, deepening the creases in his anguished frown.

"I'm sorry, Jimmy," Eva whispered. "Did you know him?"

"You don't understand," Jimmy hissed. "I..." He couldn't bring himself to explain. "There must be somebody else here." He was frantic. "Somebody who worked with Professor Wilson. Maybe they'll be able to—"

"NJ7 arrested everybody else," Eva explained. "We're the only people here."

Jimmy was struggling to keep his concentration. He couldn't take his eyes off the body on the floor and the way the man's fists were twisted into his chest.

"Jimmy, listen," Eva insisted. "I don't have long. I'm risking my life talking to you."

Jimmy was confused. Why was Eva saying that? They both knew already that NJ7 were watching. But then Jimmy doubted himself. There was something strange about the way Eva was speaking. Did Eva want NJ7 to think she was helping Jimmy or tricking him? Were they even really being watched at all?

"I waited here for you," Eva went on. Jimmy's brain was doing somersaults trying to work out the possibilities of what plan Eva was following – and whose. "You're not safe, but I'm on your side now."

I know, Jimmy wanted to shout at the top of his voice. *Why did you come here just to tell me this? And why did you warn me about the cameras?* All he could do was stare at his friend, baffled. There was something in Eva's eyes. Her expression was blank and she'd forced back her tears, but behind all that Jimmy could see an intensity he couldn't understand. It was as if she was trying to beam a thought from her eyes directly into Jimmy's head, but Jimmy had no idea what it was.

"You came to meet Professor Wilson," Eva said, her voice quivering now. "So shake his hand."

Now Jimmy was even more confused. Had Eva gone crazy? Perhaps waiting in this small office with a dead body had sent her into some kind of hysteria. She walked to the door and turned back to fix Jimmy with one last stare.

"Shake his hand, Jimmy," she insisted. "You'll know what to do then."

Jimmy watched her leave, hardly able to move until the click of her footsteps up the corridor had faded away. Finally, he turned back to the body. *Shake his hand?*

He dropped to one knee, peering closely at the

body. Could this man have saved him? The thought flew into his head. *Forget that*, he ordered himself. *I'll find another way.* Then he spotted something that distracted him from all those other worries. There was something sticking out of Professor Wilson's right fist – a sliver of green.

Jimmy leaned in closer, trying to block out the man's wildly staring eyes. The body was still warm. Jimmy could feel it as he came closer, and Wilson's cologne wafted up. Jimmy could taste it at the back of his throat. Still wrestling with his disgust, Jimmy gripped the tip of the green sliver in his fingertips and pulled it away. Wilson's fist gave it up easily – whatever this was, it obviously hadn't been in the Professor's hand when he died. That was probably just the place Eva had chosen to hide it. But was it Eva, Jimmy asked himself, or NJ7?

"You'll know what to do," Eva had said.

Jimmy stared at the object in his palm: a green flash drive. He couldn't help letting out a bitter laugh and muttering to himself, "A green stripe."

11 RATE OF DILAPIDATION

Jimmy hurried away from the institute. The wooded lanes seemed to close in around him, stifling his thoughts. He tried to maintain a steady jog, but he could feel his muscles throbbing, almost begging for a fight. On top of that, he still had only socks on his feet and his eyes wouldn't keep still. An ambush could come from anywhere. If NJ7 had been watching him, surely they'd take this opportunity to try to kill him. There were no cars around and the only buildings were huge mansions set back from the road and shielded by high walls or thick foliage. When the attack came, nobody would know about it except Jimmy.

Eva had told him that he'd know what to do, and now that seemed pretty simple – find a computer, plug in the flash drive and see what was on it. He'd dismissed the thought of using the computers at the institute. Any second another team of gunmen could arrive and Jimmy didn't plan to make their jobs even easier by sitting at a keyboard in the next office waiting for them. Instead, he'd slipped under the blind and escaped out of the window, back into the twilight.

He hadn't even worked out where he should go. The flash drive was clenched in his fist. He considered breaking into the next house he came to and 'borrowing' a computer for a few minutes, but it went against every instinct: the occupants would certainly call the police and that would bring trouble. Maybe Eva had somehow managed to stop NJ7 following him away from the institute and, if she had, stumbling into a local house was only going to undo her work.

Jimmy tensed at the sound of a car speeding towards him from behind. The engine sounded powerful – a deep, even growl that mingled with the rumble of the tyres on the road. Jimmy would have immediately jumped for cover, but the noise stirred something in his memory. He felt his legs slowing him down before he even knew why. How could he possibly identify that this car wasn't a threat just from the sound of the engine?

He cautiously glanced over his shoulder. As soon as he did, he realised that this was no ordinary car. The sound of a Bentley Arnage T gliding along a country road was unmistakable – once heard, never forgotten. And Jimmy would certainly never forget the only man he knew who owned a Bentley – Christopher Viggo. He'd stolen the car from the French Embassy thirteen years before when he'd needed some fast transport in which to escape from NJ7.

Jimmy slowed to a walk and couldn't help smiling as the sleek body of the navy Bentley decelerated to keep pace with him. It looked in much better shape than the last time Jimmy had seen it, when it had been covered in dents and scratches. The window of the passenger seat lowered and the driver peered across.

"You know not to accept lifts from strange men, right?" It was Viggo, just as Jimmy had expected.

"You got nothing better to do than fix up your car?" Jimmy asked. "This thing was junk last time I saw it. And didn't it use to be green?"

"Are we going to talk all night or are you getting in?"

Jimmy grinned and jumped into the passenger seat. He couldn't believe he was back with Christopher Viggo. It brought up so many questions he didn't know where to start. All he could do was smile at the man and stare. But Viggo wasn't smiling back.

"What's going on, Jimmy?" he barked, powering the Bentley round the curves of the road. He reached into the inside pocket of his jacket and flicked a folded up piece of paper at Jimmy. "What's all this about?"

Jimmy unfolded the paper and found himself staring at a printed sheet of numbers, graphs and names of chemicals with some scribbled comments in a box at the bottom. Before Jimmy could work out what it was, Viggo spoke again, the tension in his voice obvious. "The doctor gave it to me," he explained.

"The doctor?" Jimmy gasped. "You mean Professor Wilson?"

"No – the doctor at the hospital. The one who had you bandaged up and trapped in a deserted ward on the top floor. Or don't you remember?"

Jimmy didn't know what to say and his confusion showed.

"He and I had a little chat," Viggo explained, "just before he…" Viggo's voice dropped away for a second and he took a deep breath. "I was too late to stop NJ7 doing… whatever they did to him, and maybe he deserved it if he gave you over to them. But he had enough strength left to tell me what he'd told them, plus a little bit more when he realised I was a friend of yours. I think he genuinely felt sorry for betraying you. He kept mumbling about how he didn't realise you'd have human emotions. Wasted his dying breath saying sorry."

"Dying breath?" Jimmy whispered, suddenly cold. There was an awkward silence for a moment.

"I'm sorry, Jimmy," shrugged Viggo eventually. "I'll never be much good at breaking bad news."

Jimmy fought back his emotions, trying to make sense of what was happening. So two men had died because of him that night. A doctor and a professor.

"How did you know I was even there in the first place?" he asked, struggling to stop his voice wavering.

"I saw you on a news report," Viggo explained. "After the explosion at the tower block they were showing all the casualties being taken into the hospital." He glanced across the car with a glint in his eye. "You have to be careful where you put that face, Jimmy. You might get burned."

"Very funny," said Jimmy, without a smile.

"You were only on the screen for a split-second," Viggo went on, "but you're lucky nobody at NJ7 spotted you. They had to wait for the tip-off from the doctor. Otherwise they would have had you killed while you were still unconscious."

Of course, Jimmy thought. He had a vague memory of seeing the news crew outside the hospital, but he'd been so close to blacking out he hadn't had the presence of mind to hide from the cameras.

"Come on!" Viggo startled Jimmy out of his thoughts. "What's that piece of paper all about?"

"I don't know," Jimmy replied meekly. His eyes ran up and down the page, hardly taking anything in. "You're the one who gave it to me."

"And I got it from the doctor at the hospital. He was desperate for you to know that he'd managed to hide it from NJ7. So it must be important. What's all that stuff at the bottom about the 'rate of decay', or something...?"

Jimmy squinted at the loopy handwriting at the bottom of the page. It was hard to make out the words because the paper was thin and there wasn't enough light. The first time he read it, it still made no sense, until he realised what it was.

"He tested my blood," Jimmy gasped. "He actually tested me..." Jimmy's hand started to tremble. The blue haze at his finger tips shimmered in the dim light as if his own body was mocking him.

"What are you talking about?" Viggo asked impatiently.

Jimmy's words tumbled out in a rush as he read the doctor's notes.

"I gave the doctor a blood sample," he explained. "To run tests on. When I found out he'd called NJ7, I assumed he hadn't done the tests, but he must have changed his mind or something. Because these are the results."

"Tests for what?" asked Viggo. "What's—"

"Radiation poisoning," Jimmy cut in. Viggo's face twisted in shock, but Jimmy carried on before his friend could say anything. "It's a long story. The French tricked me. I got poisoned and I should be dead by now, but I'm not. And according to this..." His eyes scoured the test results again, every word and statistic taking on new meaning. He felt a hot rush of blood to his face.

"It said something about the rate of decay..." said Viggo. "What's that?"

Jimmy ran his finger along the doctor's notes, but he was taking too long for Viggo. The man snatched the paper back and held it against the steering wheel, flicking his eyes between the words and the road.

"The 'rate of dilapidation'," he corrected himself. "It says it's much slower than it should be. Jimmy, it says you should be dead by now, but only a low percentage of your cells are reproducing erratically." He read some more, while trying to concentrate on driving. "It says something about an 'extended latent phase'... Jimmy..." His voice brightened. "It says at this rate you could survive for some time!"

"Some time?" Jimmy repeated, grabbing the paper back. "How much time?"

"That's all it says: 'some time'."

"What?" Jimmy shouted, his electrifying joy colliding with a potent fury. "How *much* time?! And what can I do to cure it?! This is useless!" He slammed his palm against the dashboard.

"What's your problem Jimmy?" Viggo yelled. "You've just been told you're not dying. Get over it."

Jimmy had never felt such powerful and conflicting emotions. "I am dying," he insisted, between gritted teeth. "All this says is that I'm dying slowly."

"So join the rest of us," Viggo shot back. "Welcome to the human race: dying slowly is the only thing everybody has in common."

Jimmy shut his eyes for a second, as if that would blank out Viggo's voice. But there was one word that would always cut straight through to Jimmy's nerves: *human*. Slowly Jimmy began to understand what it was that bothered him so much. The test results had forced him to come face to face with the fact that he was living the nightmare of discovering he wasn't entirely human, but without the benefit of being invulnerable. It was yet another piece of his destiny that he couldn't control, and it didn't look like there were any doctors who could help him without getting killed.

"I'm sorry, Jimmy," Viggo whispered. "I didn't mean..."

"It's OK," said Jimmy, at last able to calm himself a little.

"You'll cheer up when you see the others."

The others? Jimmy thought. Then it hit him with an inner explosion of genuine elation: his mum, his sister and Felix.

"They're with you?" he asked, almost bouncing in his seat. Viggo nodded. "I knew it! Are they OK?"

"They miss you," Viggo replied, a slight smile breaking through. "But apart from that..."

"When can I see them?"

"Where do you think we're going now?" Viggo chuckled. He slammed his foot even harder on the accelerator and the Bentley's 7-litre twin-turbocharged V8 engine responded with a purr that pushed them effortlessly forwards.

"And what about Saffron?" Jimmy asked cautiously. The last time he'd seen Viggo's girlfriend, she'd been bleeding to death from an NJ7 bullet.

"She's fine too." For the first time a genuine smile stretched across Viggo's face. Jimmy punched the air in triumph. He was so excited about seeing everybody again that he almost forgot about the strip of plastic that was gripped in his fist.

"Do you have a computer?" he asked at last.

"Of course," Viggo replied. "Why?"

"I saw Eva," Jimmy explained, holding out the flash drive.

Viggo glanced from Jimmy's hand to his face. "Eva?" he gasped. "Did she give you this?"

Jimmy didn't need to say anything. Suddenly, Viggo slammed on the brakes and veered over to the side of the road. They were still out in London's suburbs, but the streets were more built up now and they came to rest under a lamp-post.

"If Eva gave you this," said Viggo, fiddling with the air-conditioning controls on the dashboard, "she's managed to get something out of NJ7 that we have to see. And that means we have to see it right now."

He twisted one more dial, which caused a catch to click, and the whole central section of the dashboard opened up. Viggo reached in and pulled out a laptop. Jimmy was impressed and couldn't hide it.

"When I was redoing the bodywork on the car," Viggo explained, "it turned out this thing has secret compartments all over the place. I think there must be some I haven't even found yet."

He hurriedly started up the laptop and took the flash drive from Jimmy.

"Wait," said Jimmy. "What if it's..."

"Booby-trapped?" Viggo pursed his lips and shook his head slightly. "Don't you trust Eva?"

"I do," Jimmy insisted. "Of course I do." He wanted to

sound sure, but his voice gave away his doubt. "It's just that, I don't know... she was trying to tell me something when she gave it to me."

"What?"

"I don't know. She couldn't really say anything, in case it gave away that we're still on the same side. We were being watched."

"Cameras?"

Jimmy nodded.

"Jimmy." Viggo sighed and ran his hands through his hair, obviously trying to weigh up all of the risks. "If NJ7 were watching you, why didn't they follow you from the institute? Why didn't they..." he tailed off.

"I know, I know," said Jimmy. "Why didn't they try to kill me then if they could obviously see where I was?"

"Maybe they couldn't," Viggo suggested. "Trust me, if they could have, they would have."

Jimmy knew that was true, but something didn't add up. He couldn't puzzle it out, and there was an insistent voice in his head telling him that perhaps the answer would be on this flash drive. He quickly gestured to Viggo to plug it in.

As soon as the drive connected, a video screen popped up. Even with the grainy image, Jimmy immediately recognised his so-called father. The frozen image of Ian Coates made Jimmy feel like a firework had gone off in his belly. Fear, anger and uncertainty fizzed through him, mixed with the old feelings of familiarity that he desperately wished would die.

Jimmy's father was sitting behind a table, with the shoulders of the people next to him just visible at the edges of the shot. It looked like a smartly decorated room, but that's all Jimmy could establish from what was on the screen.

"Hit 'play'," Jimmy insisted impatiently, unable to tear his eyes from the screen.

With one click from Viggo, Ian Coates burst into life. His eyes seemed to bulge in his head and he swayed from side to side in his chair as if he might keel over at any moment. But it wasn't the action that was so disturbing, it was the sound. There were only muffled voices at first, but then Ian Coates' voice cut through clearly.

"We're blowing up a tower block," he said.

Jimmy leaned in closer to the laptop's speakers, unable to believe what he'd just heard.

"We're blowing up the tower block on Walnut Tree Walk!" Ian Coates shouted. He slammed the table with his fist, causing the picture to judder slightly. "If anybody has any problem with that, they can leave the room now!"

That was the end of the video clip.

Eva held herself upright as she strode away from the institute building, even though she felt like crumbling. She pulled her coat around her, wishing it could make her disappear completely. Outside the gate she broke into a run. Twenty metres up the Ridgeway a long, black car slowed to a crawl and the rear door was pushed open. Eva dived in and the car pulled off again without ever having to come to a complete stop.

The warmth of the car was stifling. Eva had never had to fight so hard to hold back tears, but now it mattered more than ever that she reveal nothing of her emotions.

"Did he find it?" came a low voice from the front passenger seat. Eva was trembling too hard to answer at first. "Did he believe you were helping him?" the woman in the front asked sternly. She turned in her seat and Eva found herself fixed by a glare from Miss Bennett. "Did he fall for it?"

All Eva could do was nod.

12 THE CORPORATION

Jimmy and Viggo were both speechless. Viggo played the clip again, and even after that neither of them knew what to say. Viggo started the video a third time.

"Enough!" Jimmy snapped. He pushed Viggo's hand away and stopped playback.

"I can't believe it," Viggo whispered, all the colour gone from his face. "I knew the Government was evil, but this... this is psychotic."

Jimmy couldn't stop staring at the slightly blurred freeze-frame on Ian Coates' face. It seemed to be sneering at him.

"I..." Jimmy couldn't get any more words out. His chest was heaving, having to strain for every breath.

"It's OK, Jimmy," Viggo tried to reassure him. "He's not your father. He's just..."

"He *is* my father!" Jimmy shouted. "I might not have his blood, but he brought me up. And he's definitely Georgie's father. I can't believe he'd do this! Why would he do it?" Jimmy couldn't control his rage. "And why would Eva show me this? *Why* would she..." He tailed off and ended by slamming the lid of the laptop shut.

Viggo grabbed him by the shoulders. "Eva knew it would be hard for you to see this," he said, keeping his voice low and calm. "Of course she did. That's probably what she wanted to tell you and couldn't. But she also knew you were the only person who could do what has to be done with this video."

"What do you mean, 'what has to be done'?" Even as Jimmy asked the question, he realised what the answer was. There was only one thing they could do with this – make sure as many people as possible saw it. "We need to get this on to the Internet," he whispered. "When people know—"

"Not the Internet, Jimmy," Viggo interrupted. "NJ7 will shut it down one site at a time. A few people will see it, but the impact would be minimal." He pulled a mobile phone from his pocket and dialled a number. "We need to put this where millions of people can see it in one go. This is what I've been waiting for since the day I left NJ7." He pressed the phone up against his ear. "This could bring down the Government. We need to get this broadcast on TV."

At first Jimmy's anger at his father was overwhelmed by his excitement. Viggo was right – if they could get this clip to be shown on TV even once, it would be too late for NJ7 to cover it up. Jimmy knew how tightly the TV stations were controlled, so it wasn't going to be easy, but he could already feel his head buzzing, possibilities swirling around, joining together to create a plan of how it could be done. Then his thoughts shifted. His heartbeat slowed. Those doubts rumbled inside him again.

"Chris," said Jimmy softly, but Viggo was already talking on the phone, arranging with somebody to meet them tonight. "Chris, this isn't right."

Viggo ended his call and looked at Jimmy, confused.

"What if NJ7 wanted me to have this?" Jimmy asked.

Viggo shrugged. "All that means is that somebody at NJ7 has realised what we knew already: Neo-democracy has to be ended. It's no mystery, Jimmy. We even know who the person at NJ7 is – Eva. She filmed this and knew straight away that she had to smuggle it out to the rest of the world somehow. And you were the best person to give it to if she wanted to make sure it was safe."

Jimmy knew what Viggo was saying made sense, but still he couldn't dismiss his suspicions. *Relax*, he urged himself. He only felt uneasy because he'd been used so many times in the past. But this was different. This involved his friend, and whatever her motives, the evidence was in front of him. Ian Coates had ordered the destruction of a London tower block. He'd tried to murder his own people, presumably so he could blame it on the French.

In any case, it didn't look like Jimmy was going to have much choice about this. Viggo had clearly made up his mind. He'd started the car and was already pulling out into the road, accelerating at an amazing rate.

"Listen, Jimmy," he said, putting his foot down even harder. "It looks like your family reunion is going to have to wait." Jimmy shot him a questioning look. "I've told Saffron to meet us. She's already working on this."

"On what?" Jimmy didn't understand. Why couldn't they go to see his family straightaway?

"Jimmy," Viggo's voice was insistent, even a little impatient. "We can't waste any time. It's already getting late. If we wait any longer, everybody will be asleep and nobody will be watching TV. And by tomorrow we might have missed our chance." The lights of the dashboard reflected in his eyes, making him look even more focused. "You've found the one piece of evidence that could finally make this country a real democracy again."

Jimmy didn't see why democracy couldn't wait until after he'd seen his family, but he could tell Viggo wasn't going to be persuaded. "Whatever," he said with a shrug.

"Whatever?!" Viggo blasted. He slammed his palm against the steering wheel in frustration. "This isn't 'whatever,' Jimmy. This is democracy! Don't you care that your country is being run by a lunatic?"

Jimmy felt the sudden sting of tears prickling his eyes. He turned his face to the window and watched the boarded-up buildings flashing by. When Jimmy didn't answer, Viggo filled the silence.

"I'm sorry," he muttered. "I know you want to see the

others. But for all we know NJ7 have already found out that video clip has been leaked and right now they're doubling all of the security round Corporation facilities. That's anywhere we could possibly get it seen by the public. They'd shut down the whole of the Internet and cut TV transmission completely."

"What?" Jimmy was astounded.

"They'd do it, as well. The Government wants to stay in power that badly, they'll simply tell the Corporation to pull the plug on every communications system in the country and nobody could stop them."

"They really control *everything*?" Jimmy asked. He'd heard about the Corporation, and he'd always known about Government censorship, but he'd never realised their grip on what the public saw and read was so strong.

"They wouldn't be able to keep power if the Corporation didn't control people's access to information, Jimmy." Viggo sucked in a long breath through his teeth and muttered to himself, "Sometimes I think that's all power is."

Viggo's foot hardly left the accelerator. He powered the Bentley along side streets and blind alleys, expertly twisting through a maze of minor roads towards the centre of London. All Jimmy could do was marvel at the man's control and navigation. They didn't just avoid traffic; Jimmy realised they were travelling along the route monitored by fewest cameras. He was beginning to see how the Government's greatest enemy could travel through its capital city without being caught.

Within a few minutes they pulled into an underground car park and finally had to slow down when they reached the security barrier. Jimmy was sure they'd be caught on video now, but straightaway he noticed the security camera had been knocked off target. All it could possibly be recording were the wheels of the car. Then the barrier simply lifted to let them pass. Only then did Jimmy spot a tiny laser scanner fastened to the security bar with an elastic band.

"It's crude," said Viggo, obviously guessing what Jimmy was thinking, "but it works for a while. And by the time they discover all this and fix it, I've found a dozen other safe points where I can disappear for a few hours."

Jimmy wondered whether he would have known how to do something similar himself. Maybe his programming would have guided him to an even better solution, he thought. At the same time, it was difficult to weigh up his natural assassin instincts against the experience of a man who'd lived on the run for much longer than he had.

From here it was a short walk to the rendezvous with Saffron – at a greasy spoon café. The place was closed for the night, but when Viggo tapped on the window a light came on and a muscly young man unlocked the door. He greeted them with only a nod before disappearing into the kitchens.

"You must be a regular," Jimmy muttered.

"A friend in the right place can be more effective than a weapon sometimes," Viggo explained.

"Any chance of a fry-up?" Jimmy's stomach growled.

"Kitchen's closed."

Before Jimmy could react there was another tap on the window, in the same rhythm as Viggo's. It was Saffron, but she wasn't alone. When Viggo unlocked the door to let in the newcomers, Jimmy thought the dim light was playing tricks on him. The second person was his mum.

"Jimmy!" Helen Coates cried out, rushing to hug him.

"I thought we could use an extra pair of hands on this one," Saffron explained.

Jimmy let his mum's arms squeeze him until he thought his eyes were going to pop out of his head. Inside, he was numb. He could hear the sound of Saffron and Viggo talking softly, but he was oblivious to their words. It was a full minute before he was able to press enough strength into his arms to hug his mum back.

Eventually she let him go and held him at arm's length, drinking in every bit of him with her eyes.

"Your face!" she gasped, bringing her fingers up to the burns on Jimmy's cheek.

"Mum!" he protested, pulling away. He'd almost forgotten he was so burned, but it seemed that the skin was still raw to the touch.

"What happened?" asked Helen.

Jimmy didn't know where to start. He was tempted to roll up his sleeve and show her that it wasn't just his face, but at the last moment he realised there were probably several things she didn't need to know about – not yet at least.

"Nothing," he said. "Just forgot to put suncream on."

His mum shoved him in the shoulder. "Don't try to be clever with me, mate." She broke into a huge smile and pulled him close for another hug. "We missed your birthday," she whispered.

That was the first time Jimmy felt something cutting through his numbness. It was a sour twist in his chest that made him want to break down in a heap on the floor. Only the warmth of his mother's embrace kept him upright. He pushed his face into her shoulder to stop himself crying.

"Sorry to cut in," said Viggo. Jimmy was startled and felt his muscles tensing up again, holding back his feelings. "Can we save the emotional stuff for later?" Viggo went on. "We don't have a lot of time."

"Hey Jimmy," added Saffron. "Chris said you didn't have any shoes." She tossed him a pair of old trainers and went back to setting out maps, diagrams, scheduling charts and photographs on one of the tables. Then she pulled out a black briefcase containing computer equipment and a huge rucksack full of what looked like survival kit.

"What is all this?" asked Jimmy, keen to distract himself from the prickling in his eyes.

"This is the Corporation," she explained. "They control the only TV transmitters in the country. Every programme is sent back to one of these transmitters so it can be broadcast across the country. Our best chance of getting the video clip seen on TV is to go straight to where the output is broadcast from. The nearest transmitter is on the roof of Corporation House." She prodded a point on a map. "Regent Street."

Jimmy looked across the photographs of the building set out in front of him.

"It would be easier to hijack one of their vans," he suggested. "You know, like the ones they had outside the hospital for the news report."

"It wouldn't do any good," Saffron replied. "Whatever we did in the van would still have to go through one of the Corporation transmitters if we wanted anybody to see it. We might have control of their van, but they'd still decide whether we got on to anybody's TV screen or not. That's why we have to hit them at Corporation House, and hit them fast."

Jimmy's mind was whirring, relieved to be thinking about something other than being reunited with his mother. But he couldn't see how this was going to work.

"Even if we get into the building," he said, "how are we going to make them put the video clip on TV? I might be able to work out how to use the equipment. I mean, probably, with my... you know..."

"It's OK, Jimmy," Viggo reassured him. "We won't need to use the equipment."

"Hold on," Helen cut in. "It sounds like we're going to have to hold a whole studio hostage."

Viggo tipped his head from side to side. "We might have to..." He paused, searching for the right words. "...persuade one or two people to work for us, on a temporary basis."

"They'll shoot us," Helen declared, obviously aware of the shock value her words would have. "This is the Corporation. It may as well be NJ7's private TV company. We're not talking about the Disney Channel here."

"What's the Disney Channel?" Jimmy asked.

"Never mind," said Helen.

"Actually," Viggo muttered, "the Disney Channel would probably shoot us too if we tried anything like what we're about to do."

"OK," said Saffron, holding her hands up. "Shooting us before we've completed the job is the extreme scenario. But hopefully it won't come to that. I think if we act quickly enough they'll have to respond before they realise exactly what's going on. First, they're more likely to cut the power to the studio, or sabotage transmission some other way." She thought for a second. "*Then* they'll shoot us."

"I don't think Jimmy should be doing this," said Helen quickly. "He can go back to London Bridge. Where he'll be safe."

"London Bridge?" asked Jimmy. "What's there?"

"At the moment," Viggo explained, "just Felix and Georgie. They're in a safe place in the tunnels underneath London Bridge Station. It's where we're based for now."

"And it's where you're going back to in a minute," said Jimmy's mother. "I'll take you."

"Wait," said Viggo, with a quick glance at Saffron. "I think we're going to need him."

"He's only..." Helen didn't finish her sentence. It was obvious to everybody that it made no sense to mention Jimmy's age. Viggo and Helen were former NJ7 agents and Saffron had been trained to a similar standard, but none of them were capable of some of the things Jimmy had done.

"Like you said," Viggo whispered, looking intently into Helen's eyes. "This is the Corporation. It's going to take all four of us."

Jimmy hated being talked about as if he wasn't there. "Mum, I've..." He wanted to describe some of the things he'd had to do since they last saw each other. He'd blown up an oil rig, destroyed a uranium mine, survived two plane crashes, several explosions, the mountains and the desert. And they were just the first things that came to mind. But he held back. Those things would only add to his mum's worry, even though they were over now.

At last Helen announced what she was thinking. "Show me the plan, then I'll decide whether Jimmy comes with us."

Viggo looked from Jimmy to Helen and back. "Maybe

first you should watch the clip," he said. "Then you'll—"

"I don't want to see it," snapped Helen. "I don't need to. Let's sort out this plan, then I'll decide whether Jimmy is a part of it." From her tone, it was obvious that the discussion was over. She turned to the papers on the table.

"OK," announced Saffron, leaning over the documents. "Here's what I think we should do..."

"Be careful with my car," said Viggo, handing Helen the keys.

"Be careful with my son," was the reply.

Nobody needed to say anything else, but Helen gave Jimmy a last embrace, and a final glare to Viggo. Then she drove the Bentley, alone, out to the power substation at Clapham. It had been a while since she'd been active as a Secret Service operative, but she drove swiftly and it took her only moments to break into the substation. The chain cutters in the back of the Bentley helped too.

The floodlight left nowhere to hide, and within seconds the night guard spotted her on the security camera. But before he could reach for his walkie-talkie, Helen was already in his booth. She ran up behind him so quickly he couldn't even spin in his chair before Helen seized his wrist and twisted it over his head. The only sounds were three clear cracks of the man's bones snapping. Helen pressed her hand over his mouth to stifle his cry and lowered him gently to the floor as he passed out from the pain.

In less than a minute, she applied the chain cutters to one of the giant transformer boxes and made tiny adjustments to the rusting controls on the machinery. It wasn't much, but it was easily enough to trigger the system to regulate itself by compensating in other areas of the grid.

Now all Helen Coates could do was drive back to the rendezvous point, turn on the TV and wait for the others to join her. Phase one of the plan had been completed.

13 WHAT'S UP, DOC?

Jimmy, Viggo and Saffron huddled across the street outside the Corporation building at the end of Regent Street. It was past nine o'clock and the few people out on the street were hurrying home, as if London air carried some kind of disease at night. *Get home quickly*, thought Jimmy, watching them. *There's some great TV on tonight.*

"There it is," whispered Viggo quickly, nodding up at one of the street lights. Jimmy noticed it too: a slight flicker that told them this section of the grid had automatically switched the source of its power to an alternative substation – a standard failsafe mechanism designed to maintain a seemingly uninterrupted service in the event of a local failure in the grid.

"How long now?" asked Viggo.

Saffron gave a tiny shrug. She had kept her eyes at street level, watching the stretch of road down the side of the Corporation building. Jimmy peered impatiently in that direction too, conscious of how exposed they were.

"I thought this was meant to be an instant response unit," Viggo muttered.

"The signal is instant," Saffron replied. "The electricians were probably having a couple of drinks."

Finally a grubby blue van rolled into view, coming up the side road.

"OK," said Saffron. The three of them moved in perfect synchrony, panning out across the T-junction. Jimmy walked straight down the middle, waving his hands above his head. Two men stared out of the front windscreen at Jimmy, bafflement on their faces. The van was forced to slow almost to a halt. Before it even came to rest, Saffron and Viggo jumped from the shadows on either side of the van. They pulled the doors open and heaved the two men from their seats.

It hardly took any force at all – the shock did most of the work. One of the electricians tried to shout for help, but Viggo gave him a sharp slap across the face, which put an end to the resistance before it started. Viggo handed his electrician to Jimmy, while he jumped into the van and backed it up on to the kerb. Once the road was clear, Jimmy and Saffron dragged the workmen by the collar of their overalls and secured them in the back of the van.

Everything happened with effortless speed. People passed by along the main road, but the ambush was carried out so calmly and quietly that nobody thought anything was amiss. Even when a couple of cars came up the side road and waited at the T-junction, the drivers didn't notice what was going on, and within seconds everything was happening out of sight, in the back of the van.

"Overalls," Saffron ordered. "Boots too." Her voice was soft but commanding. The men seemed almost hypnotised and rushed to obey.

Jimmy felt a nasty thrill surging through him. Deep inside he was aware of a shred of pity for these men. The only thing they'd done wrong was to accept this evening shift as on-call emergency electricians for the Corporation. *They must be afraid*, he thought. *They must think we might kill them*. But that sympathy quickly detached itself from Jimmy's brain and withered, and he began to see the two men as lumps of meat, not people.

Jimmy tossed one set of overalls and a pair of boots to Viggo. Saffron put on the other set, and they shrugged their backpacks on over their overalls. The two electricians instinctively raised their hands, shivering in T-shirts and underpants. Viggo quickly found two tool bags and a coil of power leads in piles of equipment in the van. They used the leads to tie up the electricians and a length of gaffer tape went over the men's mouths.

The slamming of the van doors hit Jimmy like a slap in the face and brought him back to his senses. He'd just taken two men hostage. They were tied up and trapped. He couldn't shake the image of the terror on their faces from his mind.

"They'll be fine," whispered Viggo, seeing Jimmy's concern. "Come on, we've got a job to do." He picked up his tool bag and threw the second one to Saffron, then slammed the door shut and pocketed the keys. Together they marched off towards the Corporation building. Jimmy hurried behind them, still numb.

He kept telling himself that none of this violence was his fault. If his father hadn't blown up a tower block, Jimmy wouldn't have to terrorise innocent people in order to get that video clip on to the TV. He repeated it in his head over and over, but still couldn't force himself to accept that these actions were justified. Then he felt another jolt of power. His system flicked aside all of his worries and the question of whether this was justified evaporated. His programming didn't care.

Jimmy hung back while Saffron and Viggo swept through the revolving doors at the main entrance of the Corporation building. He knew his task perfectly. His muscles were primed for it, his blood pumping. Just before the door stopped spinning, Jimmy slipped in, keeping so low to the ground he was almost sliding.

Viggo and Saffron were at the security desk, holding the attention of both guards.

"We've come to look at the internal power relay in Studio 60," said Viggo in a low voice, avoiding eye contact to minimise the chance of being recognised.

He and Saffron simultaneously pulled out the swipe cards that extended on elastic cords from the belt loops of their overalls. They waved them in the air once, then straightaway let them snap back to their hips.

"These won't work out of hours," Saffron announced. "You'll need to override the internal door locks on the fifth floor." She tapped the side of one guard's monitor as she spoke. Everything was designed to prevent the guards actually examining the swipe cards, which bore the headshots of two electricians who were older, whiter and more male than the pair currently trying to gain entry to the building.

The distraction worked perfectly. The guards looked at each other, their brows furrowed. "I don't think that..." one of them began, but Viggo interjected.

"Sorry we're late. We've been tied up." He drummed his fingers on the desk, another distraction. "According to our beepers you had a power blip a few minutes ago. That's right?" Viggo nodded firmly at them and in unison the guards nodded back. "And the call went out for the electrics team. That's right?" Again, the guards could only nod. The force and monotony of Viggo's questions were conditioning them to it, along with the forceful downward jerk of his head with everything he said. "So we need urgent access to the fifth floor. That's right." This time it wasn't a question, and he didn't wait for an answer. "Have a great night."

He and Saffron moved quickly but calmly past the

desk towards the lifts. There was already a lift waiting, with one passenger inside, lurking out of sight by the panel of buttons.

"That took long enough," said Jimmy. He let the doors close and pressed the button for the fifth floor.

"I hate doing that," Viggo muttered. "I'd rather just..." He clenched his fists.

"Relax," Saffron ordered. "It worked."

"We think it worked," Viggo replied. "Until they realise they never checked our ID and they see that the names of tonight's on-shift electricians are two blokes."

"By then we'll be out of here," Jimmy cut in. He could feel his muscles thrumming, ready to complete the operation, while his brain fought the same doubts as Viggo. So many times before, Jimmy had relied on his strength and his combat skills. But tonight that would only get them so far. It might enable them to fight their way out, if they needed to, but to get the video clip on to the TV was going to take delicate strategy and timing.

The lift slowed down as they reached the fifth floor.

"Remember," said Viggo, drawing a deep breath, "don't wait. Do your job, then get out. We'll meet back at London Bridge Station."

"I'll have the kettle on," whispered Saffron as the lift doors opened.

Morrey Levy had worked as a producer and director of

TV news broadcasts for nearly fifteen years. Tonight he was in the same position he found himself in almost every night: on the edge of his seat in a bunker-like control room, his eyes flicking around a wall of almost fifty small TV screens. Around him was the focused bustle of his production team, a dozen people rushing to follow every command. At his fingertips was the main desk, a huge bank of faders and buttons.

The screen in the centre of the wall was marked OUTPUT and displayed what was actually being broadcast. At that moment it was the familiar sight of two shiny-faced news anchors next to each other in front of a garishly designed studio.

"Go three," Levy ordered into his microphone, with a click of his fingers. The output screen flicked to a view from a different camera, a close-up of one of the newsreaders. "Ready VT... Roll VT..." He clicked again and the output switched to a pre-recorded report from the wreckage of Walnut Tree Walk. Just then, the door to the control room clicked open.

"Who are they?" barked Levy, glancing over his shoulder at Viggo and Saffron. "Get them out of here! This isn't an open day."

"Sir," said one of the technicians nervously, "they're the on-call electricians. Security buzzed us about them."

"Electricians?" Levy spat out the word as if he was trying to chew his own cheek. "Get out!" He flicked his hand in the direction of Viggo and Saffron. "I don't have time for this. I'm running a broadcast." He turned back to the monitors, not bothering to see how these two interlopers were responding to his welcome. "This is going out into the homes of millions of people. You think I want you around making a fuss over some tiny glitch that didn't even register on the desks? Go back home. We don't need you. We don't have any problems with the internal..."

He couldn't finish. The cold blade pressing on his Adam's apple was too much of a distraction.

"You do now," whispered Viggo, holding the knife steady with one hand while his other was clamped on the back of Levy's head. After a second he backed away and kicked Levy's chair, spinning him round so the two men faced each other.

For the first time, Levy saw that his entire control room staff had been lined up, facing the opposite wall, with their hands on the backs of their heads.

"How did you...?" he gasped. Then he narrowed his eyes and studied Viggo's face. "You're Christopher Viggo."

"Put this video clip on TV," Viggo demanded, nodding towards Saffron, who held out a flash drive. Levy's face lit up with excitement.

"This is fantastic," he beamed. "What a story! Christopher Viggo himself finally captured trying to hijack one of *my* broadcasts."

"Shut up and get it on to people's screens," Viggo insisted, turning the knife round and punching the handle into Levy's chin. Blood seeped on to Levy's lips, but it didn't stop him smiling as his imagination swept on.

"Yes..." he pondered. "An exclusive... Captured and possibly even killed in the ensuing gunplay." His eyes glinted. "I don't mind a bit of blood on my control desk. All adds colour to the story."

"Take the flash drive!" Viggo shouted. "Cut the news programme and run the clip!"

"Listen, mate," Levy replied with a slight chuckle. "I'd help you if I could. I really would." He leaned forward slightly and lowered his voice. "I'm not as much of a fan of this Government as you might think. If it weren't for censorship, I'd be producing comedy sketch shows. But honestly," he threw up his hands in a show of helplessness. "I can't help you. It would never work. You see, live TV isn't actually live any more. There's a three minute delay to stop anything going out that's against Corporation policy."

"You mean anything the Government doesn't like," Viggo sneered.

"Whatever you call it, it doesn't matter." Levy winced and his voice trembled. "Because you can force me to put your clip on, but it won't be broadcast for three minutes, which means anybody in this studio will have those three minutes to cut it again before it reaches anybody's TV. All I have to do is hit that." He jerked a thumb towards the corner of the control desk where there was a red button protected by a flip cover. "And you can't wait around here for three minutes because security will be on their way since the last report finished and the news carried on without anybody directing it. They should be here any second. Three more minutes and there'll be a whole army coming up that corridor."

Viggo breathed deeply, absorbing all of this information. "You mean," he said, "we would have to force you to broadcast our message and then stay here for three minutes, just to make sure you didn't cut it before it actually went out?"

"That's right," Levy grinned. "And no one can override the system. You've lost."

"Well, how long do you think we've been talking?"

"Two minutes and fifty eight seconds," Saffron cut in. Her voice was totally calm. She was standing at the door, her eyes fixed on a stopwatch in her palm.

"Looks like we didn't need to override the system," said Viggo with a small smile, glancing over Levy's shoulder. Levy spun round in horror. The screen marked 'output' was no longer showing a news report, or even any footage from the studio. Instead, there was a slightly grainy film of the Prime Minister pounding his fist on a table. When the clip was finished, it looped back and started again.

"What?" screamed Levy. He lurched for the red button, but Viggo had complete control over him. He pulled the chair away and the man hit the floor with a bump. "Security!" Levy yelled. But it was too late. The clip was being broadcast.

"Let's get out of here," said Viggo firmly.

Saffron pulled open the door. The sign on the outside read 'Control Room: Studio 60' and swarming up the corridor towards them was a phalanx of security guards. But Viggo looked past them, to the other end of the corridor. There, he just caught sight of a shadow darting for the stairs. The door it had come from slammed shut. The sign on that door said, 'Control Room: Studio 59'.

Saffron flicked her flash drive on to the control desk and twisted to defend herself from the guards. Later, when Secret Service experts examined the flash drive, they found that the only video footage on it was a Bugs Bunny cartoon.

14 POWER AND LOYALTY

Jimmy sped away from Studio 59, hurtling up the stairs of the Corporation building three at a time. He slipped the green flash drive – the one from Eva – into his pocket. The crashing of hundreds of heavy boots echoed up to him, mixing with panicked shouts. It filled Jimmy with such joy that it could have been music. It meant he had succeeded. The clip of Ian Coates ordering the bombing of Walnut Tree Walk had been broadcast across the nation and now Corporation security was trying to reclaim control of their own studios.

Jimmy burst out on to the roof, relishing the cool night air against his skin. He couldn't help peering over the edge of the building. The place was surrounded. Police vans and long black cars formed a ring several vehicles deep.

Jimmy sprinted round the edge of the building, weaving between the vents. The whole roof was dominated by the giant structure in the centre – the transmitter. It towered up into the sky, its full height only visible because of the flashing light at the top. It was almost exactly the same shape as the Eiffel Tower and about half the size. This was the transmitter that sent the Corporation's TV signal around the southern half of the country and to a handful of similar transmitters that relayed it across the rest of Britain. And for a few vital seconds, Jimmy thought to himself with pride, he had taken control of it.

The control room of Studio 59 had been empty and the distraction in the studio next door had allowed Jimmy to work calmly, unnoticed by anybody. At first he'd been overwhelmed by the scale of the production console, but very quickly the faders and monitors had twisted in his mind into the shapes of basic building blocks, revealing the paths of their circuitry. In essence, the studio's operating system was very simple. It was designed that way: to allow creative TV producers and executives to control their shows with limited technical expertise. It had been no challenge to Jimmy's programming.

When he reached the other side of the building Jimmy peered into the darkness and waved his arm above his head. Straight away a silhouette on the roof of the next building waved back. He couldn't help breaking into a huge smile. Even with everything that had happened to him, he'd never expected to be escaping from the roof of the Corporation with his mum's help.

Helen Coates hurled one end of a multi-fibre climbing rope across the divide between the buildings. It uncoiled and landed at Jimmy's feet. Tied on to the end were three loops of nylon – a hand-strap each for Jimmy, Saffron and Viggo. Jimmy knew he needed to get higher so he could slide down the rope to safety.

His body was already responding. He held the end of the rope over his shoulder and heaved himself up the struts of the transmitter like he'd broken into a giant's adventure playground. His muscles throbbed with energy. It almost felt as if his biceps were growing thicker.

Despite the wind blustering round the legs of his trousers, Jimmy's hands and feet moved in perfect co-ordination. At times he was balanced on only one point of contact. As soon as the rope was taut between the two buildings, Jimmy tied up the end on one of the horizontal struts of the transmitter. At first his fingers felt clumsy, struggling in the cold and still marked by severe burns. But his blood soon brought a core of stability through his hands. They stopped trembling. The interlocking fibres of the rope moved exactly as he wanted, twisting round the metal into the simple but robust form of a perfect buntline hitch knot.

He slipped his wrist through one of the loops and gripped the upper part of it with both hands, then pushed himself off with a mighty kick. Suddenly, he was swooping through the sky. The pace of his slide stole the breath from his lungs and he thought his stomach must have been left behind on the transmitter. Every tiny irregularity in the rope juddered through him, jarring his shoulder sockets and digging the nylon hand-strap harder into his wrists.

Before he knew it, his feet dragged against the landing zone. He tucked up his knees and had to scrabble for control. He nearly scraped all the skin from the front of his legs, then ended up flat on his back, staring at the stars.

"Jimmy, you did it!" Helen's words took a second to reach his consciousness. She heaved him up and pulled him into a tight squeeze, ruffling his hair.

"It worked?" Jimmy asked, pulling his face free from his mum's shoulder.

"Look," said his mum. She let him go and picked up a mobile phone that was resting on top of her bag of equipment. "It's still going out." The phone was streaming live TV, and the image of Ian Coates pounding the table flickered across the screen. The footage was all too familiar to Jimmy now. He was almost numb to it. But when he looked back up at his mum, her smile had disappeared.

"He's crazy," she whispered, a crack in her voice. "I never knew he could..." She turned away and wiped her eyes.

"Mum, it's OK," said Jimmy, but he sounded far from sure of himself. With a burst of anger he snatched the phone from her hands. His mother was startled, but Jimmy could see he'd done the right thing. She needed to be focused on helping Viggo and Saffron.

In fact, that was the moment Jimmy caught sight of the two figures scurrying across the roof of Corporation House.

"Get out of here, Jimmy," said Helen. "I have to stay for Chris and Saffron, but you get back to London Bridge. Do you know where to go?"

"I saw it on the map." Jimmy wanted to protest and wait with his mum for the others. He knew their escape must have been much harder than his, and that Security Forces would have chased them up to the roof. But it looked like Viggo and Saffron had enough time to make it to the rope – they were already climbing the transmitter.

Jimmy ran down the fire escape and slipped away behind the backs of hundreds of Security Forces, police and NJ7 agents.

Mitchell finally decided he'd had enough of the SAS combat simulator on his PS8 console. His thumbs were aching and made him wonder how he could play for so long without noticing the time passing. He threw the controls to the floor and kicked the console off at the switch on the wall. His underground room at NJ7 HQ may have been stocked with luxuries that no other British teenager had access to, but after so long stuck here waiting for a mission, it felt like a cage.

Mitchell prowled the room, wondering whether he should go for a run or try to beat his personal best for non-stop sit-ups. It was almost a minute before he noticed the images that had replaced the combat simulator on his TV screen. When he did, he froze. He was immediately transported back to that meeting at Number 10 Downing Street. It was as if his own memory had somehow been captured and re-enacted on the screen.

At last he forced himself to move. He rushed to the TV remote control. *Surely this isn't actually on TV*, he thought. He flicked through the buttons, desperately trying to figure out what had gone wrong with his entertainment system. But there was nothing wrong with it.

He dashed out of the room, still clutching the remote, and tore through the corridors of NJ7. He felt the slap of cold concrete on his bare feet.

"Miss Bennett!" he yelled, his voice booming through the passageways. He twisted past NJ7 workers, pushing them out of the way to make it to Miss Bennett's office. At last he rounded the corner into her room. As usual when he confronted Miss Bennett, he felt that stab of insecurity in his stomach.

"On the TV!" he announced. "He's on... the Prime Minister..."

Miss Bennett's smile made Mitchell's voice choke in his throat. She was leaning back in her chair, behind her large, leather-topped desk.

"Join us," she said calmly, extending a hand to an empty chair opposite. Only then did Mitchell notice that

Eva was there too. He cautiously took a seat next to her, trying to gauge from her expression what was going on. Eva looked either confused or frightened. He couldn't work out which.

"But—" Mitchell tried again to explain what he'd seen. Miss Bennett raised a finger to cut him off.

"Don't worry," she whispered. "That's all easily explained." She ran her thumb over her bottom lip, thinking for a moment. "I'm glad you're here, Mitchell," she purred. "Eva and I were just having a little chat about loyalty."

Mitchell knew he'd never been good at working out what Miss Bennett was up to, but now more than ever she had him transfixed and confused. Didn't she care that somebody had filmed the Cabinet meeting? Or that the film had been put out on TV? Especially when NJ7 was responsible for what the Corporation broadcast, and that meant that Miss Bennett...

Finally, Mitchell realised what was happening. He felt an ice cold trickle down his neck. He couldn't stop looking into Miss Bennett's eyes, two sparkling balls of wickedness.

"You put that film on TV?" he gasped.

"No, no, no," replied Miss Bennett. She stood up slowly and moved round her desk, speaking softly and clearly. "It's impossible to say that. Or, more importantly, it's impossible to prove that. No – Jimmy Coates somehow managed to get hold of that video clip and managed to beat Corporation security." There was a gleam of delight in her face. "This country can't have a weak Prime Minister," she went on. "And Ian Coates is very, very ill. The latest reports from the hospital are not encouraging I'm afraid." She pouted a little, putting on a look of exaggerated sadness. "Which means power will pass to the new generation of Neo-democratic leaders." She leaned on the desk and bent forwards, bringing her face so close to Mitchell's he could see the perfect line of her eye make-up. "It's my generation now. If you like," she added with a smile, "it's a very quiet revolution. And I want you two to be a part of it." She turned to Eva and broke into a huge smile. "You've been extremely helpful – both of you."

Miss Bennett extended a finger and pushed a stray hair from Eva's face. Mitchell felt an unexpected rush of emotion, but couldn't identify it. Excitement? Jealousy? Miss Bennett drew out the long, thin green clip from her own hair. She inclined her head and seemed to drift into a dream as she transferred the clip to Eva, pinning the girl's hair into a neat, stylish arrangement just like her own.

"Your loyalty will not be forgotten," said Miss Bennett dreamily. "Loyalty to NJ7." Her voice took on a harsher edge. "Loyalty to me."

15 EAT IT

Mitchell saw Eva's lips trembling and suddenly felt the urge to barge Miss Bennett away from her. The only thing that stopped him was the sound of panting at the entrance to the office. Mitchell twisted in his chair to see the elongated frame of William Lee bent almost double in the doorway, supporting himself on the wall.

"How did a camera get into that meeting?" he demanded.

Miss Bennett hadn't bothered to look up yet. She finished tidying Eva's hair before calmly replying, "We'll need to look into that, won't we?"

"Look into it?" Lee raged, slowly getting his breath back. "Somebody needs to—"

"Is Corporation House back under control?" Miss Bennett interrupted.

"Yes, but Viggo got away."

"Did you say Viggo?" Miss Bennett asked, almost simpering.

"Christopher Viggo." Lee spat the name violently. "Him and his friends. The boy, Jimmy Coates, was one of them."

"Oh, so it was *them*," Miss Bennett gasped. "They're the ones who put this horrible video on the TV..."

Mitchell was staggered at how easily Miss Bennett disguised her emotions. At the same time she was able to flash her eyes at Mitchell, then at Eva, as if they were sharing a secret. Mitchell felt a rush of confidence, but hated himself for it.

"It's more than horrible," Lee scowled. "It's treason." He ran his hands through his hair, looking for a moment as if he was going to tear it all out. "I've ordered the Corporation to shut down all TV transmission and the Internet. I've taken down the mobile phone networks as well, but now people are coming out on to the streets. They're not happy, Miss Bennett. There could be riots!"

"I presume the police and the army are already on alert...?" said Miss Bennett calmly.

"Of course," replied Lee. "But I need..." He paused, took a deep breath, then his gaze settled on Mitchell.

"Me?" said Mitchell, taken aback. "I can't stop a riot."

"Maybe not," Lee snapped. "But you're not doing any good sitting here, are you?"

Mitchell turned to Miss Bennett, unsure what he was allowed to do. She gave him permission to leave, nodding firmly and waving him away. He tried to make eye contact with Eva as he left, but she held herself still, staring at her notepad and pen.

As soon as Mitchell and William Lee were out of Miss Bennett's office, Lee set a quick pace, marching along the corridor.

"What was Miss Bennett saying to you?" Lee whispered. Mitchell was shocked.

"What do you mean?"

"Come on!" Lee growled. "I know she was talking to you and Eva about something. I could hear her. Voices travel for miles along these tunnels. I would have heard everything for myself if I'd come a few seconds earlier."

Mitchell's head was suddenly a swirling mess. His mouth opened, but words refused to form.

"Never mind," Lee grumbled eventually. "You weren't designed to talk, were you?" Again, Mitchell didn't know how to respond. The dim strip lights of the corridor seemed to seep into his brain, stopping him from grasping exactly what was going on. Part of him was pre-occupied trying to picture what was happening on the streets above his head.

"Are there really riots?" Mitchell asked.

"Not yet," muttered Lee. "But forget about that, Mitchell. It's not your problem."

"But I thought..." Mitchell was even more confused.

"I'm not sending you out on to the street," Lee explained. "Using you to stop rioting would be a tragic waste of your unique... disposition. That was just to get you away from Miss Bennett." At last a smile crept on to his face. "She's been keeping you on a leash, hasn't she?"

"I s'pose." Mitchell could feel his gut roaring, something in his programming jumping at the thought of finally getting into action.

They rounded one last corner and Mitchell found himself in a part of the NJ7 network he hadn't seen before – a huge laboratory. Dozens of technicians in white coats were moving bottles and liquids around, that Mitchell assumed were chemicals of some kind, and the whole room was full of the whine of the computers that lined the walls.

"I'm going to give you what you deserve." Lee put his hand on Mitchell's shoulder and brought him over to one of the computers. "A mission."

Jimmy hurried through the streets. He'd never seen London like this. There were no cars clogging up the junction at Oxford Circus. There was very little noise. Then, one by one or in small groups, people appeared to fill up the pavements and roads. They didn't seem to be going anywhere, and they weren't saying anything to each other, but they were scowling. Some of them were wiping away tears or openly crying.

A nasty tingle crept through Jimmy's flesh. He thought this might be how a wild animal felt when it knew a storm was coming. He kept his head down, avoiding eye contact, and hurried south towards Piccadilly Circus. But as more and more people came on to the street, he couldn't help knocking against them to make his way through the crowds. It was eerily quiet.

He wouldn't usually have pulled out a mobile phone surrounded by so many hostile looking people, but his curiosity was too strong. As soon as he looked at the screen of the phone he noticed there was no coverage for calls. Was that coincidence, or was NJ7 trying to stop people who'd seen the TV broadcast spreading the news to those who hadn't? Jimmy wanted to check what was on the main channels, but when he opened that function on his phone, there was simply a blank screen, with the time in the corner. It was the same on every channel. After a few seconds it was replaced by a Union Jack. There was no sound to go with it. The Corporation had nothing to show.

Around Jimmy was a low murmur of voices, steadily growing, then a few isolated shouts. Most people were heading in the same direction now, washing Jimmy along with them. He realised they were heading towards Westminster, and the Houses of Parliament. Suddenly, the sound of glass breaking smashed the silence. Straightaway there was a second crash.

Jimmy picked up his pace. He could almost smell the anger. The air was heavy with it. The crowds were made up of people of all ages, but even the other kids had looks on their faces as angry as any adult. Jimmy saw a boy about his age who was walking alongside his father, copying the man's shouts.

"Get him out!" he grunted, and others were shouting it too. Jimmy assumed they were talking about the Prime Minister, and getting him out of office, but there was something more to their words – a physical power. It was as if they wanted to drag Ian Coates through the streets. A homeless man was burning a newspaper with the Prime Minister's photo on the front.

Jimmy clenched his fists and forced back a lump in his throat. He pressed on, weaving through the crowds, letting his shoulders buffet the people around him as if he could knock away his own emotions. Then he reached Piccadilly Circus, where people were spilling out over the roads. The glare of the huge neon hoardings flickered on people's faces, lighting them in bright reds and greens that changed with the displays.

Jimmy wanted to break away from the crowd, but before he could force his way through, the street lights went out. Then the lights in the shop windows. Finally, a second later, every neon sign that covered the walls of every building round Piccadilly Circus shut down. London was cast into blackness.

William Lee brought Mitchell to one of the computer stations in the NJ7 lab. Mitchell could feel the rush of exhilaration that came with any mission. Finally, he thought, he was going to be allowed to do what he did best – what he was made for.

"We've traced the poison," Lee began, his eyes shifting around the room to check on the activities of the scientists.

"Poison?" Mitchell blurted out. "I don't..."

"Come on!" Lee hissed. "Get your brain switched on. The poison that sent Ian Coates to the hospital."

Mitchell nodded hurriedly, while Lee drew a pair of latex gloves from a box and put them on.

"We tested everything that Ian Coates might possibly have come into contact with before he collapsed," Lee went on. "In the end it was something quite simple, but the best assassinations are always simple, aren't they?" He lowered his face and stepped closer to Mitchell, who shrunk a little in the shadow of this giant.

"You mean assassination attempt," Mitchell muttered, "don't you?"

"Of course," Lee conceded, with a leering grin. "We all hope that Ian makes a full recovery." There was an awkward pause while Lee signalled to one of the lab technicians, who hurried over, bringing a small plastic pot. "We traced the poison to this," Lee declared, showing it to Mitchell.

Mitchell's exhilaration seemed to freeze in his veins. Lee was showing him a small, plastic, see-through pot, containing a single, pale white cube about the size of a large dice. The label gave away what it was, and what presumably Ian Coates had eaten. Even though Mitchell didn't speak Icelandic, the label didn't need translating. He recognised it straightaway.

"Shark meat," announced Lee. "From Reykjavik, Iceland."

Mitchell didn't know how to react. He knew that the raw, untreated meat of a Greenland shark was highly toxic. Icelanders traditionally buried it for months before it was fit to eat. More importantly, Mitchell also knew how that particular tub of shark meat – *raw* shark meat – had come to be in London.

"You were in Reykjavik, weren't you?" Lee asked.

"Yes." Mitchell's voice came out louder than he'd expected and several technicians turned to look at him. "I was tracking Zafi, the French assassin. I followed her to Reykjavik. She was in the market and I nearly…" Mitchell's memory of that fight was strong. He could almost taste the salt in the air, and feel the crunch of Zafi's bones against his fists. "She got away," he murmured.

"But she didn't get away with any shark meat, did she?" Lee furrowed his brow and examined Mitchell's reaction. "I've read the Reykjavik police report from that incident. It says that after the fight there was shark meat all over the floor of the market." He waited for Mitchell to respond, but he didn't, so Lee pushed further. "Raw shark meat. Enough to easily fill a tub about this size."

Mitchell stared up at Lee. A part of him longed to shrivel away and disappear, but that part was crushed by the urge to split Lee's chin with a single uppercut.

"Yes," Mitchell growled, having trouble finding his

voice. "I brought the shark meat to London. I was obeying orders. I didn't know how it would be used. I didn't know—"

"It's OK," Lee reassured him, seeing the violence flare in Mitchell's eyes. "That's what I'd assumed. How could you possibly have known what it was going to be used for? And I know there's no point asking who ordered you to bring it," Lee continued. "Was it a text?"

Mitchell nodded.

"Of course," said Lee. "So anybody with access to NJ7 encryption and communication could have made it look like the order was coming from someone else."

"So..." Mitchell began, but Lee held up a hand to stop him.

"I just want you to say sorry," he explained, with a casual shrug.

"Sorry?" Mitchell was puzzled. Lee nodded, so Mitchell said it again, more firmly: "Sorry." It still didn't sound sincere, but Lee didn't seem bothered.

"I forgive you," he said, with a glint in his eye. "Now eat it." He held the tub out to Mitchell, who stared first at the white cube, then up at Lee, then back at the tub. "Eat it," Lee repeated, more firmly.

"But..." Mitchell could feel his body preparing to strike. He saw exit routes from the lab flash through his mind. He saw Lee's blood spurting from his nose and ears. He saw the bodies of all the technicians.

"Don't you want to?" Lee simpered. Mitchell was

disgusted by him. Lee may not have had Mitchell's strength, but he was revelling in his authority. They were the tactics of a bully.

At last, Lee sighed and pulled the tub away again. Had he seen in Mitchell's eyes how close he'd come to being savagely attacked? "Well, in that case..." Lee twirled the tub in his fingertips, glaring at Mitchell, then turned to the computer and tapped a few keys. A window came up showing a search in progress. "My team finally found a partial fingerprint on this tub that didn't match the PM's."

"Whose is it?" Mitchell grunted, a rising fear gripping his lungs.

"That's what we're about to find out," replied Lee. "This is a search of the internal NJ7 database. Every agent, former agent and staff member is in it, as well as every member of the Government and civil service. So are their fingerprints." Mitchell watched the 'percentage completed' number rise in the search window, while Lee rattled on. "There's a different database for the general public, of course," he explained, "but searching that would take much longer and I'm confident this will give us a positive result."

As the number on the screen approached 100, Mitchell's anxiety grew. In his mind, every possibility was slowing ticking round as he tried to work out what Lee was trying to achieve by bringing him here. Then at last Lee explained.

"Quite simply, Mitchell," he said with a sigh, "the person who took the poison to the Prime Minister is about to appear on this computer. So that's your mission: kill whoever's face comes up on this screen."

Mitchell's insides twisted into a whirlwind of turmoil. The assassin in him was taking hold of every muscle, sending a devilish delight through his mind. At the same time, Mitchell's human fear burned stronger and brighter. He knew exactly whose face was going to appear. He remembered his trip to Iceland just as he remembered every day since he'd discovered he was a genetically designed assassin. And in all of that time only one woman had been in control of his orders. Others had taken a hand in training him and supporting him, but only one person had instructed him to bring the shark meat back to London. There was no way those instructions could have come from anybody else. His new target was surely Miss Bennett.

Mitchell was suddenly aware that Lee was still talking to him, giving him further details about how he was to go about his mission, making sure to complete it in total secrecy. He couldn't trust anybody at NJ7. Everybody was a possible threat. But Mitchell's mind was miles ahead of Lee. The risks were already pounding through every thought. Of all the targets in the world, surely there was nobody more dangerous to take on than Miss Bennett.

She may not have had even a fraction of the combat training that infused Mitchell's blood, yet still he couldn't be in the same room as her without feeling totally under her power.

I can't do it, he heard himself thinking, followed immediately by a roar that seemed to blast away the whole room, yet he knew was only inside his head. *I must*, he heard, *I will. It's my mission. My life*. Then, finally, the computer screen showed a new message: search completed. Next to it was a face – the face of Mitchell's new target.

Eva Doren.

16 POWER AND CONTROL

Jimmy knew the sudden darkness was no accident. In the same instant a wail of sirens went up in the streets all around him. The blue flashes were like flames flickering up the wall of Piccadilly Circus. London was in lockdown.

Jimmy held himself tense, his senses twitching, ready to protect himself wherever violence broke out. His night vision quickly surged into action, casting the whole city in a blue haze and giving everybody on the street the look of a zombie with glowing blue eyes. People were flowing in from every direction, and for a few seconds they stumbled into each other, some of them stopping, but very quickly they found mobile phones or lighters to see by, and the wave moved on.

Jimmy pushed through the mass of angry people, desperate to reach a side street, or anywhere he could move more quickly to reach London Bridge. But as he battled across the central reservation of Piccadilly Circus, past the statue of Eros, he realised why it was so hard to move freely. He smelled the horses first, and knew what it meant before he saw them: the cordon of mounted police and armed crowd control units.

They were trying to manage the flow of people, blocking off the side streets to keep everybody where they wanted them – either Trafalgar Square was already dangerously overcrowded or the police were simply blocking the route to Westminster. Jimmy felt the crowd surging in different directions, like a single beast, but there was nowhere for it to go. He ducked down and tried burrowing between people, but he was quickly even deeper in the pack, surrounded by shuffling feet.

Then a few of the feet started stamping. There were more sirens, more flashes of blue, more shouts, colliding with each other and rising up into a roar. And Jimmy knew that any second the roar would erupt into a riot.

Mitchell felt a wrench in his stomach and his mouth went dry. The sounds of the room seemed distant, detached. He barely heard William Lee muttering, "Well, Eva Doren. I have to admit I'm surprised, but never mind. If she's the one responsible for poisoning the PM, she's the one you have to kill. Unless you want to try some of this raw shark meat yourself?"

The words echoed around Mitchell's skull. He couldn't muster enough power to think the order away. "But..." he gasped at last. Lee wasn't interested.

"Make it quick," he said. "She's young." With that, he stalked away, checking on the rest of the work being done by the NJ7 technicians. Mitchell stood in front of the computer, staring at the headshot of Eva. It was a standard NJ7 identity picture, but to Mitchell, Eva still managed to have a sharp look while somehow looking vulnerable at the same time.

How could she possibly be responsible for poisoning Ian Coates? Mitchell eventually forced his muscles to unfreeze and moved back through the corridors. He could feel his whole body fizzing with a black energy. His programming was driving it through him, preparing him to kill. He tried to contain it, but the struggle only increased its intensity. Before he realised it, he found himself running through NJ7's passageways, the beat of murder drumming in his heart.

There's something wrong, he told himself. *Eva didn't do this.* Mitchell's brain felt like it was twisting in on itself, trying to wring out some kind of clarity while his programming grew in strength. He thought back to Reykjavik, to the fight with Zafi and the order from Miss Bennett to bring the shark meat to London. She'd said she wanted to analyse it – to understand Zafi's methods. More and more details were coming back to Mitchell now. There was no way Eva could have been behind the assassination attempt on the PM. *She's being used*, Mitchell realised. *Like I was. It has to be Miss Bennett.*

The tunnels of NJ7 seemed to be closing in around

him as he ran. He was close now – any second he would come to Miss Bennett's office. All he needed was to reach her before he saw Eva. Then he could force her to explain what was going on. She could give him fresh orders. But at the same time Mitchell had no idea how his programming would respond if Eva was there as well. Would he have the strength to resist completing the mission William Lee had just given him?

He sprinted round the last corner. Immediately, his worst fears were confirmed. Walking up the corridor towards him on the way out of Miss Bennett's office, sorting out a handful of notes, was Eva.

"Oh," she said, looking up. "Mitchell." There was a light in her expression that was completely out of place in these dark halls. It wrenched Mitchell's gut. His killing instinct responded with a surge so powerful that for a second he couldn't breathe.

"You OK?" asked Eva, still smiling softly. Mitchell couldn't remember the last time anybody had looked pleased to see him. But that joy was smashed by another blast of violence in his bloodstream. He was ready to kill.

When Eva saw Mitchell coming towards her down the corridor, she was surprised at how relaxed she felt. She couldn't let life at NJ7 become normal. If she relaxed, she might let her guard down. *He's an assassin*, she reminded herself. *He's not entirely human.* But she knew that the same was true of Jimmy, her best friend's brother. Sometimes she couldn't believe how upside-down the world had become.

She was risking her life every day by pretending to be working for NJ7. Miss Bennett trusted her now. Eva had infiltrated the heart of the world's most deadly Secret Service, a double agent, working for enemies of the Government – her friends. And yet she'd been the one to deliver that video clip to Jimmy. It had been on Miss Bennett's orders, of course, but Eva wished she'd been able to think quickly enough to warn Jimmy that it was a trick.

She walked towards Mitchell, pushing her mouth into a smile and finding that it came easily. Of all the people at NJ7, he was the one she felt most comfortable with. But then she saw the look in his eye. Her smile dissolved. Mitchell let out an anguished grunt that shocked Eva into dropping her papers.

What's he doing, she asked herself desperately. Before the thought was even finished, Mitchell was pounding towards her like a tank. *They've found me out,* Eva thought. *I'm dead.* She couldn't move. Her brain was frozen, her muscles were like brick. She couldn't even scream. All at once it felt like every cell in her body was coated in terror.

Mitchell's fist whipped up from his side so quickly that Eva felt it before she saw it. It slammed into the centre of her chest, punching all the air from her lungs. Mitchell lifted her off her feet by the shirt and slammed her against the wall. He held her there, glaring into her eyes.

"Mi... Mi..." Eva gasped, but she couldn't pull in enough breath to speak.

Mitchell raised his arm above his head, aiming for her neck, but Eva could see his pupils rapidly flicking from side to side. She knew one blow would end her life. Mitchell was built to kill and now she felt his power – in his speed and the effortless strength in his arm. But she knew he wasn't fully developed yet. There was still a human voice somewhere in his head. There had to be. If only she knew how to call to it now.

Mitchell's hand hung in the air above his head for what seemed like an age, ready to chop. Then, at last, he let out another raging moan, clenching his jaw tight. At the very bottom of Eva's dread was the hope that Mitchell's human pity was fighting for her.

"Shark meat," Mitchell grunted, forcing the words out as if his own face was refusing to speak.

"What?" Eva croaked, finally finding her voice.

"Shark meat." Mitchell's forehead was dripping with sweat. His eyes were bloodshot. He was a quivering ball of power that had nowhere to go. "That's where the poison was."

"Shark meat poisoned Ian Coates?" asked Eva, her words soft but clear.

Mitchell scrunched up his face and nodded. "You sent

it," he whispered, straining against the muscles in his own shoulder, holding back the killer blow.

"No!" Eva rushed to explain. "I remember it..." She couldn't stop tears rolling down her face. "It was in a little pot... Shark meat from Iceland..."

"Poison!" yelled Mitchell.

"I didn't know!" Eva wanted to scream now, but she knew that it could tip Mitchell over the edge and finally make him the killer he was born to be. She consciously relaxed every muscle, hanging limp in Mitchell's grasp. "Miss Bennett told me to take it to him. It was in a pile of other gifts from governments around the world..."

Finally, Eva watched the muscles in Mitchell's shoulder relax. The ball of pure strength sank and he lowered his arm. When he looked Eva in the eye again, she saw more desperation than anger – more pleading than fighting.

"I didn't know," Eva repeated in a soothing whisper. "It wasn't me." She could barely stop herself sobbing, but knew she had to be strong. Mitchell respected her – the human in him did, anyway. "I'm not your target." She could feel her body shaking, but Mitchell lowered her to the ground. The floor under her feet was one of the most wonderful sensations she'd ever experienced.

"Having trouble with your mission, Mitchell?" The whisper rushed up the corridor. Eva and Mitchell both turned quickly, like rabbits who've heard the click of a hunting rifle. At the end of the corridor, strolling slowly towards them, was the long, bean-like silhouette of William Lee.

"It wasn't Eva," Mitchell panted. "She just took the tub to the PM's study. She—"

"I know." Lee cut him off. "I heard everything. I made sure to be a little closer along the corridor this time, and to listen a little harder. I thought you might find this particular target... emotionally challenging. So I thought I'd follow you and see how things were going."

"I've done nothing wrong!" Eva was shaking. "You can't kill me!"

"No, you're right," Lee sighed. "I don't think I can. Instead, you'll bring me all Miss Bennett's secrets."

"What?"

"Her files, her modes of control, her codes, her contacts at the Corporation and everything she has planned."

Eva was frantically trying to work out what to do, but her brain was still coming down from the relief of surviving Mitchell's attack.

"She's obviously trying to use this crisis to take power. I knew she would eventually, I just didn't think she'd resort to actually poisoning the Prime Minister."

That was the first time Eva had heard it spelled out so simply: Miss Bennett had tried to kill Ian Coates. She might still succeed if things didn't go well at the hospital.

"What if..." Eva gasped.

"It's OK," smiled Lee. "She'll never be Prime Minister. Because I'm taking power."

Eva's head spun. Did nobody in the Secret Service care that the Prime Minister's life was on the line? Were they all so hungry for power?

"I'm going to run this country the way it should be run!" Lee went on, barely keeping his voice level. "I'm taking power and nobody can stop me! The British need me, Eva. Now bring me Miss Bennett's secrets so I can wipe her out!"

Eva and Mitchell were left stunned. By the time Eva shook off her fear and looked at Mitchell again, William Lee had disappeared, deep into the NJ7 tunnel system.

"He's trying to take power," she whispered, half to herself.

"So is Miss Bennett," Mitchell replied.

"Don't sound so upset about it, Mitchell dear." And there was Miss Bennett, behind them, leaning casually against the wall of the tunnel. "If Ian Coates isn't well enough to run the country, then wouldn't you rather that I did it?"

Eva and Mitchell whipped round to face her.

"But you're the one who poisoned him!" Mitchell shouted. Eva was thrilled by the strength in his voice. He was either being very brave, or very stupid. "And Eva nearly got killed for it! Now Lee wants her to steal your secrets!"

Miss Bennett bowed her head dramatically. "I know," she said. "You don't think you can have a shouting match right outside my office without me hearing, do you?" She raised an eyebrow. "That man has revealed himself to be a bit of an idiot, hasn't he?" She paused for a thought that obviously pleased her, judging by the smile on her face. "And Mitchell," she said, turning serious, "you obey orders from me, not William Lee. The only person above me is the Prime Minister, while he's still alive. So don't try to kill Eva again. It's just not nice."

Eva didn't know how to respond. If Miss Bennett had heard their conversation with Lee, she must have also heard Mitchell's attack. *Was she ever going to intervene*, Eva wondered.

"What about Lee?" Mitchell asked forcefully. "Should I..."

"Don't worry about him." Miss Bennett waved away Mitchell's concern. "If he wants to tell anybody he's taking over as Prime Minister, he'll have to use journalists, who'll have to use the press, the Internet or the TV. Unfortunately for him, those are three of my toys, and I'm not sharing."

"But he'll find some way, won't he?"

"And that is where luck is on our side." Miss Bennett stepped forwards and reached out for Eva. Eva couldn't help flinching. She realised she was still shaking from Mitchell's attack and the shock of their encounter with William Lee. But Miss Bennett gave a soft smile, as if she understood, and Eva couldn't help leaning towards her.

Miss Bennett placed one arm gently round Eva's shoulders. With her other hand, she tidied Eva's hair. She removed the green hairclip she'd put in place earlier that evening, all the time keeping her face close to Eva's, smiling like a kindly school teacher. After a few seconds she drew herself upright again and fiddled briefly with the hairclip.

"Before William Lee can say anything to anybody," she explained, "there's probably something the British public should see."

Suddenly Miss Bennett pulled out her mobile phone and inserted one end of the hairclip into a slot at its base. She held the phone up so they could all see the screen. First it flickered, then, to Eva's amazement, it showed an image of the corridor they were standing in, and William Lee. Miss Bennett squeezed something on the hairclip and the image started moving. A thin sound came with it, from the speaker in the phone.

"I'm taking power," said William Lee on the screen. Eva couldn't believe it. The hairclip contained a hidden camera and recording device.

"I'm taking power and nobody can stop me!" Lee ranted, before Miss Bennett stopped the playback. Her face was deadly serious.

"With a little editing," she muttered, "we'll make him the most hated man in Britain."

17 PUPPET SHOW

Mitchell and Eva waited until Miss Bennett's footsteps faded away. Eva could picture her stalking the NJ7 labyrinth. This was her world, and her presence seemed to hang in the air even now that she was gone. Eva marvelled at the woman's perfect manipulation of everybody around her and mentally ticked off Miss Bennett's latest achievements. She'd poisoned the Prime Minister, putting him in a critical condition in the hospital. Then she'd leaked the video of the PM to destabilise the country and turn his popularity into hatred. Now she was about to pull the rug from under her closest rival, William Lee.

She has everyone on strings, Eva thought to herself. *We're her puppets.* And soon she would be in a position to take over as Prime Minister.

"Er, listen, Eva..." It was Mitchell, stumbling over his words. Eva was so distracted that she'd almost forgotten he was there – but not that he'd been going to kill her. "I'm... you know... sorry about..."

"It's OK," said Eva bluntly. "It's not you." She was awash with a mixture of pity and anger. If Jimmy could fight against his assassin instincts, surely Mitchell should be able to as well.

"Yeah," said Mitchell, a deep frown on his face. "So, like, this is mad. Do you think Miss Bennett is going to take over? What's going to happen to us?"

Eva was about to answer that she had no idea, but suddenly a thought struck her. "Ian Coates is still alive, isn't he?" she asked.

"I think so," said Mitchell. "But last I heard he wasn't exactly—"

"Who's protecting him?" Eva's heart was pounding again and she felt a rush of urgency.

"Well, apparently there are people in the streets who are, like, chanting about him, or something, so they're keeping his location a secret and he's got guards from the army and NJ7."

"But who's protecting him from NJ7?"

"What do you mean?"

Eva didn't need to explain. In a moment, Mitchell's face changed. He'd realised it too – Miss Bennett must have chosen which NJ7 agents were guarding the Prime Minister. If they were loyal to her personally, and not to the Government, then as soon as she had undermined William Lee, she could quietly order her team to do away with Ian Coates.

"We have to get to Coates," gasped Mitchell. "Miss Bennett's agents will kill him."

Eva had come to the same conclusion, but something was bothering her. How had she suddenly found herself in this position? She was considering trying to save the life of a man she thought was an enemy.

"What's the matter?" asked Mitchell, reading her expression. Eva quickly forced a smile, but it was obviously fake. "We have to help him," Mitchell insisted. "It's our duty."

"But..." Eva hesitated, but in the end couldn't hold herself back. "That man is evil."

"He's the Prime Minister," Mitchell replied immediately. "I want to be loyal to Miss Bennett too, but she said it herself – the Prime Minister is above her. I serve him. Maybe Miss Bennett will be Prime Minister one day, when Ian Coates decides..."

"When he *decides*?" Eva was aghast. "What's the difference between Miss Bennett taking power like this and the way Ian Coates took power? He wasn't elected, was he?"

"Elected?!" Mitchell was struggling to keep his voice down. "Who wants a Prime Minister that's been elected? This is a *Neo-democracy!* You think ordinary people know more about running a country than Miss Bennett? Voting went out with the dark ages."

Eva wanted to take Mitchell by the collar and shake him. Didn't he understand what he was saying? Couldn't he see what the results of this Neo-democracy were? The Prime Minister had bombed his own people! She wanted to scream it into Mitchell's face. Then she finally realised that none of this mattered. She was faced with a simple choice: Ian Coates or Miss Bennett. Who would she rather have running the country? In a way, she thought to herself, this was her time to vote.

"You're right," she said at last. "We have to get to him before Miss Bennett puts that video on TV. Once she makes sure she's the only possible person who can take over, she'll kill him."

"That's what I've been saying!" Mitchell groaned. "Now how do we know where he is?"

"What do you mean, 'how do we know'?" scoffed Eva. "We work in the Secret Service, you idiot! And I'm the one who types up Miss Bennett's notes. Come with me."

The noise around Jimmy was punctuated by screams. People buffeted against each other violently. Jimmy couldn't see over them, but he could hear the pounding of the police riot shields and he caught sight of cricket bats and broken bottles. Where had they come from? Suddenly the whole mass of people surged to one side, as if a few at the edges had charged at the police, or been pushed back. There was no way of telling which. Then came more screams and Jimmy was nearly thrown to the ground. He just managed to regain his balance, but others around him weren't so lucky.

An old woman toppled in front of him, hitting the pavement hard. Jimmy reached out to help her up, but she pushed him away, struggled to her feet on her own, then immediately carried on shouting at the top of her voice. Even in the dim light Jimmy could see the bulging veins in her neck, taut with fury. Somebody pushed a broken snooker cue into her hand. She thrust it upwards like a tribal spear.

Has everybody gone crazy? Jimmy thought. He had never felt the accumulated rage of so many people. It was as if the whole country was crammed into that small space. The swell of the crowd took him in so many different directions he had to concentrate hard to remember which way he wanted to go. Then the whispers started.

Beneath the shouts and the clatter of protesters clashing with police, Jimmy picked up a breathless current of murmurs. "He's dead," Jimmy heard. "Coates is dead."

Jimmy stopped and squeezed against the people around him to turn, trying to see the person who had said it, but it was impossible to tell. Then came another voice from behind him. "Ian Coates is already dead..."

Immediately, Jimmy felt the sting of tears. His physical response shocked him. Should he care if Ian Coates was dead? The man had lied to him, betrayed him and tried to have him killed. But still the tears ran down Jimmy's face and he felt a burning in his chest.

It's just shock, he told himself. *Stay calm.* Still, he had to know if it was true. He tugged on the coat of the man next to him.

"What's happening?" Jimmy shouted. He could barely hear his own voice over the din. "Is Ian Coates...?"

Hearing the name, the man looked down at him. There was pure hatred in his eyes. He let out a horrible cry that hit Jimmy harder than any weapon. The words weren't clear, but Jimmy was sure he heard "kill".

This is no good, Jimmy told himself, trying to push away his panic and keep his breathing steady. *I have to know the truth.* Without the right information, he felt completely powerless. A thousand thoughts were rushing through his head. If Ian Coates was really dead, would the threat of a riot go away, or would people carry on until their anger burned out? Then he thought that perhaps the police were telling people Ian Coates was dead in an effort to keep a lid on the violence. If that was the case, it wasn't working.

Jimmy scrambled for his phone again. There had to be a way of finding out what was going on. As soon as he flipped it open, he saw that network coverage had returned. He quickly accessed the TV function. If the phone network was back up, maybe the Corporation was broadcasting something on TV as well.

He was right: at first the small screen was filled with the Union Jack again, but after a few seconds it faded out. In its place was a news studio – perhaps even the very one Viggo and Saffron had taken hostage. But that didn't matter now.

Jimmy held the phone close to his face to make out what the newsreader was saying above the noise of the crowd. Before he could catch a word, the image switched to a room that looked like one of the offices in Downing Street. The camera zoomed in on a figure standing in front of a desk. The screen on Jimmy's phone was too small to make out who it was at first, but then he recognised the person and felt a chill hit his heart.

He didn't even notice that all around him the noise was dying down. Within seconds, there was awed silence. At last Jimmy was pulled out of his shock and looked up. He dodged from side to side to try to see why everybody had stopped. He followed the gaze of the people next to him and found himself looking up at the very top of one of the buildings overlooking Piccadilly Circus. The largest advertising hoarding was broadcasting the same image that had just appeared on Jimmy's phone.

"Good evening, everybody," boomed a voice. Jimmy imagined it echoing through the whole of London – and the whole of Britain. "I'm the Director of the Secret Service."

Jimmy stared up at the face of the woman who had once been posted undercover as his form teacher. Now, to Jimmy, she represented everything that was rotten in the world.

"I'm known as Miss Bennett," she announced slowly.

A gentle smile drifted on to her face, filling the screen. It was the only light in London and nobody could take their eyes off it, least of all Jimmy.

"For a long time," she said, "my identity has been hidden. But in the last hour some new intelligence has been uncovered that I judged of the utmost importance for national security. You must all see it. That is why I have asked the Corporation to broadcast this on every channel, and your local police and fire services have been working quickly to put up big screens all over the country."

The footage cut away from Miss Bennett to show the crowds gathered round giant screens in Trafalgar Square, Charlotte Square Gardens in Edinburgh, Grey's Monument in Newcastle and a handful of other locations across Britain. Each of them looked more packed with people than the last. There was even a brief shot of Piccadilly Circus. Jimmy craned his neck to find the TV cameras, but could only make out the tops of police vans which had surrounded the crowd, with giant loudspeakers mounted on top of them. They were blasting out Miss Bennett's voice.

"It has become obvious," she continued, her face back on camera, "that the shocking video shown on Corporation One earlier this evening was a fake." There were a few murmurs from people in the crowd, but other people quickly hushed them, eager not to miss a single word of Miss Bennett's address.

"That's right," she confirmed. "It was a fake. Ian Coates

did not order the destruction of the tower block on Walnut Tree Walk. That would have been..." She paused and let out a tiny laugh. "...psychotic. No, the man in that film was an impersonator – an actor who is now in custody and is co-operating fully with our investigation. It has become clear that he was being employed by this man..."

The camera pulled out again, and as it did, Miss Bennett added, "Let me warn you that this new evidence may be disturbing to some viewers."

The screen faded to black. Then came a view of a dark tunnel, dominated by a huge man shaped like a telegraph pole. Jimmy recognised him from the news bulletin he'd seen at the hospital. After a few seconds, Jimmy remembered his name: William Lee.

"I'm taking power!" Lee ranted on the screen. The footage was grainy and a bit jerky, but his voice was perfectly clear. "I'm taking power and nobody can stop me! Get me Miss Bennett's secrets so I can wipe out the British. Now!"

The crowd erupted into howls. Some of them hurled things towards the big screen, but they landed dangerously among the other people. Then there was a sudden hush again as Miss Bennett returned to the screen. Her expression was serene, but commanding. The enormousness of the image, and the fact that it was so far above Jimmy's head, seemed to give Miss Bennett an added allure.

"You probably recognised that man," she said. "That

was William Lee, who we believed until this evening was a loyal member of Ian Coates' Government. The video he created was part of a plot by him to seize power from the Prime Minister. William Lee is now missing, believed to be on the run."

Jimmy could almost feel the words sinking into his consciousness, being spun through a rapid-fire analysis by the programming in his head.

"So it is my duty at this time," Miss Bennett went on, "to call upon each and every one of you to remain calm. We share your anger and distress at the tragic attack on Walnut Tree Walk. But Ian Coates was not to blame." Her eyes glowed even brighter, staring right into the camera, as if she could see into the hearts of every person in that crowd.

"I have asked the Corporation to broadcast a special programme of light entertainment for you, and to allow you all to access the Internet as usual. So please feel safe to return home. I will be making another address in one hour, when I will be able to update you on the recovery of our much loved Prime Minister, Ian Coates. I'm sure he is in all of our thoughts and prayers at this difficult time."

Jimmy could feel the threat of the crowd dissolving into the night. He could see everybody's shoulders drooping. Their hunger for a fight was fading.

"Finally," declared Miss Bennett, "I would like to reassure you that if any tragedy should occur, and for any reason Ian Coates is unable to resume his rightful position at the head of Government, then William Lee will certainly not be the one to take over." A few people shouted their approval. "That honour is one that I, myself, will be forced to reluctantly accept." Again, there were yells of "yeah" – a few more this time.

"Thank you for your patience, people of Britain, and, for now, goodnight."

18 VISITING HOUR

The screen faded to black, then was suddenly replaced by an advert for Marmite. One by one, the other neon displays flickered into life, like a multicoloured sunrise. The crowd was silent. It was as if they were waking up from a nightmare. A few people stared at the makeshift weapons in their hands and scratched their heads, puzzled about why they were clutching cricket bats and broken bottles. When the streetlights came back on, the police started controlling the flow of people away from Piccadilly Circus. The pace was steady – almost dreamlike.

Jimmy was as stunned as everybody else – but for different reasons. He couldn't believe Miss Bennett's performance had convinced so many people. He picked up snippets of murmured conversations. People were confused, even shocked. Not many were praising Miss Bennett, but nobody was as angry as before. *She's better than ever*, Jimmy thought to himself with horror. *Not just a teacher – a headmistress.*

Then what she had said sank in. *The video clip was a fake*, Jimmy thought. He couldn't move, he was so overwhelmed by the mixture of horror and relief in his gut. On the one hand, it meant that Ian Coates hadn't bombed the tower block after all. *Maybe he's not a monster*. Jimmy felt a surge of warmth towards his father and was desperate to push it away, but it felt like the heaviest weight he'd ever carried and it wouldn't budge.

Then there was a terror that made Jimmy's hands shake – he was the one who'd put the video clip on the TV. All of this chaos was his fault. He remembered Eva's strange expression when she'd given him the video. *Of course*, Jimmy thought. *She knew it was fake.* William Lee had forced her to give it to Jimmy and she hadn't been able to reveal the truth.

The crowd gradually dispersed, leaving Jimmy isolated in the middle of Piccadilly Circus. He felt as exposed as the naked cherub on the statue in the middle of the junction. *What an idiot*, he scolded himself, clenching his fists. He'd ignored his own doubts about the video clip and been carried away with Viggo's haste to get it on to the TV.

I have to get to London Bridge, Jimmy insisted in his head. *I have to tell them about Miss Bennett*. He felt like he was coming out of some kind of trance. Everything in his head was so foggy. Nothing made sense. *No*, he realised. *They probably saw it for themselves.*

He rubbed his face hard, unable to make sense of his thoughts. *I've been used again*, he told himself. *By a man I've never even met!* He couldn't help letting out a growl of loathing. How had he let this happen? Britain had nearly been plunged into chaos because of his stupidity. And now Miss Bennett was even more powerful. Jimmy couldn't stop himself imagining her delight at guaranteeing her position as second-in-command to Ian Coates.

If anything happens to him... Jimmy thought. Then he stopped. He looked around. Piccadilly Circus was emptying quickly. The wind whipped across the tarmac, throwing litter into elaborate curls while a stray dog scavenged in the bins. The Londoners who had been so desperate to take action only a few minutes before had filtered away, deflated. *Have they accepted her?* Jimmy asked himself. *Do they trust her?* Fragments of Miss Bennett's speech floated into his head:

"If any tragedy should occur, and for any reason Ian Coates is unable to resume his rightful position at the head of Government..." Jimmy shuddered in horror. *"That honour is one that I myself will be forced to reluctantly accept."* Slowly, the pieces were falling into place in Jimmy's head.

"She's taking over!" Jimmy said aloud.

"I will be making another address in one hour," Miss Bennett had said. Suddenly Jimmy was certain of one thing: Miss Bennett would be Prime Minister

within sixty minutes, and Ian Coates would be dead.

Unless I do something.

He felt a tidal wave of raw energy rip through him. It seemed to explode in his brain, leaving chaos. Miss Bennett had to be stopped. But Jimmy knew the only way he could do that was to help his own father.

Confusion made him shake. He felt his programming stealing that energy and directing it towards his muscles. He surged into action, pumping his legs into a sprint through the streets. *Where am I going?* he asked himself desperately. He had no idea where the Prime Minister was. He could hardly even see what was directly in front of him because of the tears welling up in his eyes.

You know already, Jimmy heard in his head. It was like trying to grasp a sliver of a dream that he'd already forgotten – just like all of his dreams. But the knowledge was there. The assassin in him knew. *The hospital,* he told himself. *Of course.*

His feet pounded on the pavement. He remembered the surprise on the faces of the agents in the hospital car park when he'd 'borrowed' the clothes he had on now. *Those agents weren't there for me,* Jimmy told himself, straining to pick up his pace now that he knew where he was heading. *They were security for the Prime Minister.* And now, Jimmy realised, Miss Bennett would use those agents not as security guards, but as assassins.

* * *

Ian Coates drifted in and out of consciousness. When he was awake his whole body burned with pain. There was still poison in his system, corroding his insides. Meanwhile, anti-venom chemicals were being pumped through his blood from a machine next to the bed. They came in a concoction so powerful, though, they were almost doing as much harm as good.

In his delirium, he found his mind twisted with torment. The toxins streaming through his brain threw up thick swirls of colour, each one darker than the last. The browns were full of hatred. The blues brought fear. The dense black was pure guilt.

Flashes of light pushed through the darkness and grew into vivid pictures before exploding and disappearing again. Some were memories from his childhood that he thought he'd forgotten. Others were moments from his family life – the life he'd destroyed. And some were scenes he could never possibly have witnessed, and wished he could never have imagined: a tower block gushing with flames. His daughter running for her life from Secret Service agents. Jimmy gasping for breath as NJ7 bullets tore through his chest.

The terror jolted him back to reality. He automatically squeezed his thumb down on the clicker that delivered more painkilling drugs to his bloodstream. It didn't seem to have any effect. He pressed the button over and over, with all the strength he could muster, but the burning in his veins only increased. He dropped the clicker and reached for the call button that was attached to the bed frame.

As Prime Minister, his treatment had involved every comfort that only the very wealthiest patients in Britain would have experienced. That included total privacy, of course – a large hospital room to himself, up on the top floor of the private wing, with stunning views of the Houses of Parliament and Big Ben, just across the Thames.

The most experienced specialists in the country were on call around the clock, with somebody posted in the waiting area immediately outside the room at all times. At the push of a button, either a doctor or a senior nurse would come running to his bedside. But no matter how many times Ian Coates pressed the call button, nobody came.

"Doctor..." he tried to shout, but his voice was so feeble he barely heard it himself. The effort made him cough and splutter. "Doctor..." he tried again, determined to get attention. This time his voice was stronger, but would never have carried beyond the walls, and it left a stabbing in his chest.

I'm the Prime Minister of Britain, he thought to himself, fighting the pain with stubborn concentration. *Why don't people come when I call?*

The blackness rose again. *No*, he thought desperately. *Don't black out.* As the world faded away from him, he doubted he would ever come round again. At the edges of his consciousness, he heard a crash outside. *Hold on*, he told himself. He tried to twist in his bed to keep his muscles awake, but even curling his fingers took a huge effort.

Then came another crash. What was happening? At last the door burst open. But what came in wasn't a medical professional. In fact, it hurtled in so fast Coates couldn't even make out whether it was human. The shock destroyed any strength he had left. As his eyelids clamped down over his eyes, he felt something pulling on the drip that connected his forearm to the machine next to the bed. He tried to muster his strength, but couldn't stop the drip being pulled out.

My medicine, he thought to himself in horror. *Without it I'll die!* At the same time, he felt the darkness in his system melting away. He opened his eyes. He still felt like there was a thick fog in the room, but it was clearing. The door was open and the light from the waiting area filtered through to his brain, seeming to bring him another level of strength.

Finally he was able to focus. What he saw through the open door made his lungs heave in a desperate gasp of air. A doctor was sitting at his post, as he was meant to, but the man's head was bent all the way backwards, over the chair. His neck was snapped.

At first Ian Coates thought it was another gruesome vision from his delirium. But the image stayed in his head as if it had scored itself into his eyeballs. He opened his mouth and this time his cry came out with the force of a head of state. "Doctor!"

"The doctor's dead," came the reply. Only now was Coates aware of the shadow over his bed. Moving awkwardly, he shifted to see a boy of about thirteen standing by him, grasping in his fist the tube that he'd just ripped from the Prime Minister's arm.

"Mitchell!" Coates gasped.

Eva had never run so hard in her life. She forced her legs to keep moving long after they would have given up, sprinting up the stairs two at a time. Mitchell had deliberately sabotaged the lift to limit the escape options for the NJ7 agents. But after that, Eva hadn't been able to keep up with him.

She reached the top floor with the crashing of Mitchell's attack still echoing through the waiting area. A violent sickness lurched in her chest when she saw the doctor draped backwards over the chair, his eyeballs rolled back into his skull. Eva pulled away, holding her face in her hands, shaking. Then she had to step over the bodies of six NJ7 agents, unconscious but not dead.

She rushed into the Prime Minister's room and was caught off guard by yet another horror. The man looked like he had aged a hundred years. His skin was so pale she could almost see the muscles and bones in his face, and his cheeks were heavily pockmarked. His hair had turned from a lush brown to the colour of dust and he was covered in sweat.

For a few seconds Eva couldn't help seeing Ian Coates not as the Prime Minister who had done so much to keep Britain in a state of fear, but as the father of her best friend – a friend she missed and feared for more than anybody in the world.

"He's going to be fine," said Mitchell calmly. He was busy punching keys on the machine Coates had been attached to and reading the numbers that came up on the display screen just next to it. "The kill order only came through from Miss Bennett a few minutes ago. The doctor refused to contaminate the drugs, so they…" Mitchell waved his hand in the direction of the hallway. "They needed to find somebody else who could do it, and it looks like that took time. The poison hasn't got through his system yet."

"Poison?" gasped Ian Coates, his head shaking and his eyes rolling about the room. "Miss Bennett?"

"Prime Minister!" shouted Mitchell. "Can you hear me!"

"Are we too late?" asked Eva, rushing up to the display screen. "What does all of this mean?"

"I don't know," Mitchell replied straightaway. "I mean…" He hesitated and his face creased with doubt. "I do know, but I don't, like, know what I know. It just…"

"It's OK," whispered Eva. "I understand."

Suddenly the Prime Minister seemed to lurch into life. He grabbed Mitchell's arm and stared at him, his eyes a dark red. "What's happening?" he demanded, sounding as if he had a throat full of acid. "What are you doing?"

"We're saving your life," Mitchell replied. He pulled his arm away sharply. "According to this blood work, you were on your way to recovering before they tampered with your drugs tonight. So just keep still, keep your hands off me and you might survive."

"Keeping still might be a bit of a problem," said Eva. She was peering out of the window, not across at the moon-like face of Big Ben, but down at the water. Even on a choppy night like this one, the lines that cut through the waves were obvious. They were the tails of seven speedboats tearing across the Thames from the opposite bank. They were like black sharks, only distinguishable from the water because of their wake catching the light.

"Get away from the window," Mitchell ordered. With simple, bold movements he pulled the cords that brought down the Venetian blinds. "Turn out the lights. All the lights. In here, out there and in every room along the whole corridor. Quickly."

"If we move now, we can get him out of the hospital," Eva protested.

"It's too late," replied Mitchell, his voice low and strong. "They know their security has been breached. They're coming."

19 MESSING ABOUT ON THE RIVER

Jimmy tore through London. He didn't have time to care about being seen or caught on camera. He just had to run.

The streets were still far busier than they would usually have been at this time of night. People were wandering about, most of them confused. They had nowhere to direct their anger since Miss Bennett had told them what she wanted them to believe. So their anger was mutating into fear.

Some people were still shouting at anything and everything in the street. Either they hadn't heard Miss Bennett's message, or they didn't believe it. There was uncertainty on everybody's faces. Jimmy twisted past two bunches of young men, hassling each other and arguing. The fear and the anger created a bitter, almost violent mix.

When Jimmy came to Parliament Square, that violence was much closer to the surface. This was where the most serious protestors had come – right outside the Houses of Parliament. Unfortunately, Government supporters had converged there too. People were calling for Miss Bennett now, and many for William Lee. The names merged into one horrible sound. Jimmy had to weave his route carefully to avoid bursts of fighting. Then came the batons of the riot police. Jimmy pressed on, not looking to either side, but wincing at the grunts that punched through the shouts and screams. Each one was another blow that had met its target.

The face of Big Ben appeared to be deliberately looking away, sickened by the savagery of the people massed in the square. Even the gothic turrets of the Government building seemed to be recoiling in disgust.

That place is empty, Jimmy thought to himself, picturing the unfortunate members of parliament and civil servants who might have found themselves stuck inside. Powerless, as always. Jimmy wanted to shake every protestor and shout, *The people you want are under your feet.* That's where NJ7 was – controlling everything.

He picked up his pace and made it to Westminster Bridge. It was even busier here than in Parliament Square. Londoners streamed in both directions over the bridge, either to join the protests or to escape them. Jimmy bobbed between them, every now and then catching a glimpse of his destination: St Thomas' hospital. It looked out over the river, directly opposite the Houses of Parliament. A narrow, tree-lined street and a low wall separated it from the water.

From here it looked like the place was deserted –

every window was dark. What if his father had been moved? Or what if Miss Bennett had already succeeded and the man was dead? Jimmy elbowed his way to the side of the bridge and stopped, leaning over the handrail. His eyes scanned St Thomas'. The lights around the rest of the city had come back on now, so why was the hospital still in total darkness? Surely even if the Prime Minister wasn't there, the other patients were. No – the place was *too* dark, Jimmy thought. Something was going on.

Jimmy felt his muscles tense up. His body had made its decision, but it took a few seconds for his mind to catch up. At last he realised what the assassin in him had seen straightaway: seven shadows cutting through the water, heading across the Thames towards the hospital. Speedboats manned by NJ7 forces – small, black boats with solid hulls and sharp noses.

The cold air coming off the water bit into Jimmy's cheeks, but inside he felt a burning urgency. There was no doubt now. Ian Coates was trapped in St Thomas' Hospital and these soldiers were on their way to kill him. Jimmy didn't have time to wonder why Miss Bennett was sending so many men, or why the agents already at the hospital weren't doing the job. That would have to wait. For now, he had no choice.

Jimmy climbed up on to the handrail effortlessly and crouched, holding on to one of the ornate green lamp-posts that ran the length of the bridge. At first some of the passers-by gave him funny looks. Those looks turned into shouts when he dived out into the air.

The screams were left behind on the bridge and were mostly ignored in the confusion of everything else. Meanwhile, Jimmy seemed to hang in the air forever. The sounds of London swirled around him on the wind. He loved the rush of the world through his skin. It came with a wild fantasy: what if he could fly? Nobody would be in his way. There would be no bridge, no river – he would surge to the top of St Thomas'. *I'd be unstoppable*, he thought, closing his eyes.

For a second it felt as if all of his troubles were evaporating. He was weightless, suspended in mid-air, perfectly still, while the universe spun around him. *I'd never stop*, he heard himself thinking, stretching his arms out over his head. *If I could fly, I'd keep going, on and on, away from London, away from Europe, and I'd never come back...*

SMACK.

The impact of the Thames slapped the fantasy out of his imagination. His hands broke the surface of the water, then his head, then the rest of him plunged into the black, stinking swell. The sudden cold gripped his senses. He couldn't see anything at first, and the air in his lungs streamed out of his mouth and nose in a flurry of bubbles. In the blackness, Jimmy couldn't stop the bad memories. He'd been here before.

When NJ7 had first sent agents to take him from his

home, he'd gone on the run, without knowing who the men worked for or how he was able to overpower them again and again. At the time he could never have known what trials were ahead of him, but he remembered the pure fear and how it so quickly flowered into aggression. His powers had been waking up. Now they were stronger than ever and developing all the time.

Jimmy's jaw opened automatically and his mouth sucked in a gulp of fetid Thames water. It churned inside him, feeling as if it was filling every corner. However much he hated the bitter flavour, the ice cold sensation in his organs and the queasiness in his stomach, he knew his body was extracting the oxygen. He was breathing water and this was almost the exact spot where he had first done it when he'd jumped from a helicopter without knowing whether he would even be able to swim, let alone breathe.

He was deep in the water now, skimming the riverbed. It was thick with debris and dying plant life. Jimmy wove through it like a shark through a shipwreck. The slightest twitch of his body propelled him forwards as if he had evolved to travel through water at speed. He surged on, thrilled at his own transformation into a human torpedo. And that was exactly the effect he had when he reached the first speedboat.

A subtle twist of his hips sent Jimmy powering towards the silhouette of one of the boats, directly above him. The rapid kick of his legs accelerated like a finely tuned motor. He stretched his arms out above his head again, with his hands linked into a wrecking ball.

THUD!

Jimmy's fists punched into the belly of the first speedboat. But he didn't stop. His momentum carried him upwards, as if he was jumping straight out of the water – except the speedboat was in the way. The laws of physics did the rest. The boat leapt off the surface of the river like a bucking rodeo bull, the outboard motor squealing as it churned against thin air. The six NJ7 agents inside were caught totally by surprise. Two of them were thrown straight up into the air. The others gripped the side of the boat, thinking it would save them. But the whole thing flipped over and tossed them into the water.

Jimmy saw the successive splashes of Secret Service agents hitting the surface, then the boat crashing upside-down next to them. He couldn't stop himself smiling. He'd already plunged downwards again, without anybody seeing what had attacked.

The small fleet fanned out to cover a wider area and accelerated. Jimmy circled beneath them, waiting for the moment to strike again. There were now six fully manned attack boats still in the water, but within seconds they docked and the men disembarked.

Jimmy was impressed at how calmly they had taken the attack. It was obviously vital not to draw the attention of all the people on the bridge. Even the agents who'd been dumped into the water hadn't let out a sound. The mission had hardly been disrupted.

Jimmy could feel his programming throbbing inside him, almost merging with the rhythm of the river's currents. The same thing was happening inside him – his human self seemed to be shifting with the ebb and flow of his programming through his blood. The two were swirling together. Jimmy had no way of telling them apart, and at that moment had no desire to separate them either. He was functioning as a complete being – a totally efficient assassination unit.

He let his arms relax and floated up until he was just below the surface of the water. Now he circled again and watched. The shadows of the agents were diffracted in the water, making them look like pillars of black smoke. Jimmy waited until all the men had climbed over the low wall that separated the street from the river.

Even from under the water Jimmy could tell their body language was uncertain. Most of them were looking anxiously over the waves, studying them for the hidden menace. A few glanced towards the bridge, concerned about what the public had seen. For now the shelter of the trees along the river kept the NJ7 force out of sight of ordinary Londoners.

With an explosion of energy, Jimmy surged forwards. He glided just under the surface and thrust his head out of the water directly behind one of the boats. Before he could even cough up the water in his body and take a breath of air, he launched his attack.

He pushed himself up and planted his hands over the back end of the boat. If the agents saw him, they were too slow to react. With an almighty judder through his whole body, he flipped his legs up, out of the water and over his head. When he was completely vertical, his body jerked again. The core muscles in his stomach and along his spine were like blades on an iron propeller. His body circled over itself – but he didn't let go of the back of the boat.

At the peak of Jimmy's backflip, he lifted the speedboat out of the water and brought it with him. All he could see was a whirl of blackness, lit by the water spraying off his skin and hair. But he could feel the power in his arms making the boat feel like a heap of splinters. He landed squarely with both feet on top of the short wall, coughing and spluttering. He retched hard to bring up a lungful of black Thames water, and his first breath of air was like a new life. Yet he never stopped moving. He couldn't – he was in the midst of the NJ7 attack force.

Jimmy's arms were raised above his head, brandishing the biggest weapon he'd ever used – a speedboat. He brought it crashing down through the lower branches of the trees and swept it sideways, knocking three agents to the floor and sending three more hurrying backwards to avoid being crushed.

The other agents didn't hesitate to draw their weapons – the ones that hadn't been lost in the water. But Jimmy brought the boat back round in front of him, knocking any agent within three metres over the wall into the Thames. The others managed to fire off several rounds, but the bullets only pinged off the bottom of the speedboat. It was Jimmy's shield, bulldozer and sword, all in one. He swung it round his head, tearing a hole in the foliage above him and scattering the NJ7 force.

But they weren't defeated. Even while the agents were struggling against Jimmy's might, he saw the calm determination on their faces. These were no ordinary soldiers – this was NJ7. They were trained using the same systems that were programmed into Jimmy's blood. They knew all about him and had been warned what to expect if they ever came up against him.

The agents who had ended up in the water were climbing over the wall again now and joining the counter-attack. Even while Jimmy was hurling the speedboat around his head, he spotted the commanding glances flashing between the soldiers. Half of them peeled away and ran towards the building behind them – St Thomas' hospital. They weren't going to try to beat him, Jimmy realised. A few of them needed to hold him back for a few minutes, while the others continued their mission.

I can't let them, Jimmy thought. His programming was already working on a solution. He threw the boat directly up into the air with a hard spin and dashed a few metres up the wall to a second boat. The first boat landed with a crash, its nose on top of the wall, its back end bobbing in the Thames. Jimmy powered up the second boat and sped out into the centre of the river.

Behind him, the NJ7 agents hesitated, not believing that Jimmy was giving up and running away. Jimmy was light-headed from breathing water for so long and with an unnatural glee in his chest he had to force back a laugh. He glanced over his shoulder. Agents wearing dripping combat gear and bemused expressions were wondering whether the fight was over. *It's just starting*, thought Jimmy.

He wheeled the boat round to face the hospital again and accelerated. The engine roared into action. Jimmy willed it to full capacity. He was at the bank in seconds, but didn't stop. The boat he'd left upturned at the edge of the river acted as the perfect ramp. Jimmy aimed for it now, the breath freezing in his throat. Was this even possible?

Jimmy's boat hit the first with a crunch and lurched into the air. He skimmed the top of the short wall and sailed over the street. On either side, NJ7 agents dived out of the way. Jimmy scythed through them, leaning to his right to direct the boat towards his target: the entrance of the hospital.

The boat twisted on to its side and landed with a harsh bounce. Jimmy held on. The edge of the boat scraped across the pavement then smashed through the doors of the hospital. Jimmy instinctively threw his arms up around his face to protect himself from the flying glass. The boat screeched across the lobby of the hospital and crashed through the reception desk, sending papers flying everywhere. It finally slammed into the snack machine by the bank of lifts in an explosion of coins and crisps.

But NJ7 agents were already pounding up the stairs to find Ian Coates – and kill him.

20 THE MAKING OF A MONSTER

Eva crouched in the darkness below the window. A soft glow was creeping through the slats of the Venetian blinds. It picked out Mitchell's eyes, which glowed like a tiger's. He was crouched right next to her, so close she could feel his body rise and fall with his breathing. His head was steady, directed towards the door. He was ready to pounce at the first sign of movement.

"Thank you..." rasped Ian Coates.

"Quiet," Mitchell insisted in a whisper. "We have to listen for how many are coming and when."

He must have felt Eva trembling next to him, because he leaned towards her and added, "Stay here. Don't move unless I tell you to." His voice was soft and surprisingly deep. Eva felt the heat of his breath on her ear and didn't know whether she felt reassured or more afraid.

"Thank you for coming for me..." Coates said again. His voice was thin and so quiet that Eva could hardly make out what he was saying. He murmured something else, but it quickly faded out. Eva wasn't sure about it, but one word she picked out was "Georgie". Had the Prime Minister just addressed her as his daughter by mistake?

The wait stretched out for what seemed like hours. *We should have tried to escape*, Eva thought. The sound of her breathing merged with Mitchell's. It was all she could hear now, but she had to trust that Mitchell was sensing something more – the vibrations of other movement through the building, perhaps even the mechanism of the lift telling him whether anybody was close to the top floor. It had quickly dawned on both of them that the patients in the rest of this wing of the hospital must have been hastily moved elsewhere.

They'd both heard some kind of struggle going on at street level, but it had been hard to work out what was going on. All Eva knew was that dozens of NJ7 agents had arrived on speedboats, heading for this hospital room. Where were they?

"Is anybody—" Eva began, but Mitchell cut her off.

"Shh!" he placed a hand on hers. She was startled by how cool his fingers were. "Someone's—"

The click of the door handle cut him off. It triggered Mitchell's reactions. He shot across the room in a single leap, just as the door burst open. Eva flinched, knowing she was about to be caught up in bloody hand-to-hand combat. She cowered in the corner, unable to watch. The conflict of her thoughts was as violent as the coming battle: she finally had to admit that a part of her genuinely cared whether Mitchell would be hurt. *Why?* she asked herself in anguish. *He's my enemy!*

The silence of the ward seeped into her brain. Where were the sounds of the fight? She forced herself to turn back to the door. Mitchell had pulled back and was frozen in the centre of the room. Eva looked past him and saw the silhouette of another boy framed in the doorway, dripping wet and pouring the last crumbs of a packet of crisps down his throat: Jimmy.

"Get away from the Prime Minister," Jimmy snarled.

"We're here to save him," Mitchell barked back. "Not to kill him."

Jimmy stepped cautiously into the ward and pushed the door shut behind him. The light creeping through the Venetian blinds cast horizontal bars across his face in a dim orange. Water pooled at his feet and his knuckles were bleeding from his battles with the NJ7 forces, whose unconscious bodies now littered the whole building.

"I know what's going on," he said firmly, scrunching his crisp packet into his pocket. "Miss Bennett's taking over the country. She wants to get rid of..." He jerked his thumb towards Ian Coates, but couldn't unlock the muscles in his neck to look at the man. "She sent you with a team to finish the job."

"Think about it," Mitchell replied immediately. "If she'd

sent me, the job would be finished already. Nobody else would be necessary." His shoulders rose slightly, the bulge of his deltoids testing the fabric of his T-shirt.

Jimmy edged forwards. He could feel the tension in his hands and the force of his programming surging through to the very tips of his fingers. He was ready to strike. *Not yet*, he pleaded with himself. "Do I look convinced?" he asked, forcing the words out of his clenched jaw.

"It's true, Jimmy." Eva jumped up to stand by Mitchell. The interruption took the sting out of Jimmy's aggression and Mitchell must have noticed it. He glanced suspiciously at Eva, then back at Jimmy.

"Why do you believe her more than me?" he asked bitterly. "She's the one who betrayed you."

"And you're the one who's usually trying to ram your fist through my face," Jimmy snapped. The two boys took a half-step towards each other.

"Jimmy!" Ian Coates' hoarse whisper sliced through Jimmy's brain. His body didn't know whether to melt with joy or explode with rage. It was the sound of the man who had brought him up, joked with him, comforted him – then betrayed him, denied he was his son and issued the order to kill him.

A thousand thoughts crashed through Jimmy's head, but he couldn't make any of them out clearly. He found himself drawn towards his father's bed. The man's face was horribly disfigured, the skin scarred and pale, but his lips were drawn in a weak smile. The sight of it made Jimmy feel sick.

"You..." Jimmy rasped, his own voice failing. "How could you...?"

"What's going on, Jimmy?" Ian Coates asked at last, shifting in his bed. "Did you say that Miss Bennett is taking over the country?"

Jimmy couldn't speak. He was mesmerised by his father's face. This could have been a different man from the one he'd grown up with – far, far older. Then there was the strange expression: a half smile that grew in confidence with every second.

"Do you feel better... sir?" asked Mitchell.

Ian Coates was breathing heavily, but the colour was returning to his cheeks. He nodded slowly, without taking his eyes off Jimmy.

Suddenly, Jimmy lurched forwards. The anger in his chest bubbled over, fuelled by the overwhelming urge for violence. He landed with his knee on Ian Coates' chest and slammed one hand up into the man's chin to hold his head back. With his other hand, Jimmy slapped away the man's resistance. "I could snap your neck in an instant," Jimmy seethed.

Mitchell launched into action. Jimmy was aware of the shifting shadows as the other boy dived towards him, but Jimmy was frozen. He couldn't get out of the way and he couldn't complete his attack. He stared into his father's eyes for that split-second before Mitchell barrelled into him. Something stopped him moving, as if his muscles were locked in place – was it his programming or his human conscience?

Mitchell slammed into Jimmy with the force of a typhoon. They both tumbled off the bed and crashed to the floor. Only now did Jimmy's limbs unlock, just in time to struggle free of Mitchell's hold and push himself to his feet. The two boys held themselves opposite each other, neither one moving except for their eyes, which took in every twitch of every muscle of their opponent, ready to strike back at the first sign of counter-attack.

"So neither of you is here to kill me," said Ian Coates in a strangled whisper.

"I serve my country," said Mitchell quickly, almost automatically. He stared into Jimmy's face, but confusion flickered through his body. After the longest second of Jimmy's life, Mitchell burst into action again, aiming a kick at the side of Jimmy's head. Jimmy ducked to the side, grabbed Mitchell's ankle with both hands and used it like a monkey bar to swing himself under the Prime Minister's bed. He slid across the floor and came out on the other side of the bed, then jumped up and twisted to face his opponent, with the Prime Minister lying between them.

"Enough," Ian Coates ordered. Mitchell and Jimmy both froze.

"But... but..." Mitchell stammered.

"He's not your target," Coates insisted. "For now. If we want to stop Miss Bennett, we'll have to work together.

All of us. I need your help and you need me alive."

Mitchell dropped his eyes to the floor like a bewildered dog.

"It's OK, Mitchell," Coates explained. "Jimmy knows that if he kills me, he may as well be working for NJ7. Miss Bennett would win. That's right, isn't it, Jimmy?"

Jimmy nodded cautiously, but he knew it wasn't that simple. His human feelings were flooded with blood lust. He wanted to attack. Was it his programming holding him back? Did he have some kind of built-in respect for the Prime Minister that was stronger than his desire for revenge or for justice?

"And if Miss Bennett wins," Ian Coates went on, gradually regaining some energy, "then the person who was really behind the attack on the tower block will be free to bring havoc and destruction to the whole of Britain." He looked quickly at Mitchell, who seemed to flinch. "We don't want that, do we, Mitchell?"

Mitchell didn't answer.

"You've done terrible things," Jimmy whispered, forcing himself not to look at his father in case it triggered another attack.

"Believe me, Jimmy," replied Ian Coates. "That video of me ordering the bombing of the tower block – it was a fake." His words rushed out, almost breathlessly. "Miss Bennett – she's the one behind these horrors. She's the one really running the country. And now she wants to take over for good. We can't let her!"

Something deep in Jimmy's brain noticed the expression on Mitchell's face, as if he was going to say something, but stopped himself. Then Jimmy saw the other boy glance at Eva, who had pressed herself back against the window, her face in her hands. Jimmy was trembling, turmoil churning up his blood.

"I meant," he whispered, "you've done terrible things *to me.*"

He felt the sting of tears gathering in his eyes, but dropped his gaze to the floor to hide them. That's when he caught another glimpse of the growing blue stains around the tips of his fingers and he couldn't hold back the tears any more. For a moment there was silence.

"I'm not a bad man, Jimmy," said Ian Coates softly. "You have to believe that."

"Prove it," Jimmy growled.

There was no answer, until Eva rushed forwards and placed a hand on Jimmy's shoulder. "We have to get him out of here, Jimmy," she pleaded. "Miss Bennett isn't going to give up. She'll send more forces to kill him, then she'll take over. And the public is on her side. Look." She pulled him over to the window and pulled apart two slats of the blind.

Jimmy squinted out at the Houses of Parliament, Big Ben and the Thames. Then he saw Westminster Bridge, more packed than ever with people bustling in both directions. He couldn't hear what they were shouting, and they were too far away for him to make out their expressions, but some of them were punching the air in a regular beat. Some of them simply had their fists raised.

"She has them in the palm of her hand," Eva explained. "She'll wait until it disintegrates into total disorder, then announce that the Prime Minister is dead and take control herself. There's nothing we can do unless we get him to safety." She jerked her head towards Ian Coates.

"That won't do any good," Jimmy murmured.

"Then what?" Eva threw her hands up in despair, but Jimmy spun round with new energy.

"Listen to me," he said with confidence. "You too, Mitchell." Mitchell eyed Jimmy cautiously, but he listened as Jimmy's words whirled on. "Parked on the forecourt of the public wing of this hospital is a Corporation TV News van. I'm going to tell you a list of things. You two bring them up."

"I don't work for you," Mitchell grunted.

"Do it," Jimmy ordered. His voice was as powerful as any weapon. "We've got to finish this forever."

Jimmy turned to the window and stayed like that until long after he heard Mitchell and Eva going down in the lift. He pretended to be staring out at the world, but all he could see were the slats of the blind. The sound of his father's breathing filled his head.

"Jimmy," Ian Coates said eventually, his voice soft.

Jimmy fought to stop himself trembling with rage. "I was there," he whispered. "At the tower block."

"What?" His father sounded horrified.

"I tried to…" Jimmy's voice faded, overpowered by the memory of the heat… the flash… the total destruction.

"I tried to stop them too," said Ian Coates in a rush. "I tried to tell them it was an outrage. But Miss Bennett…"

"Shut up!" Jimmy shouted, gripping his head in his hands. He couldn't stop hearing his father's voice as he'd heard it on that recording: *"We're blowing up the tower block on Walnut Tree Walk!"*

The sound pounded through his head until the words didn't make any sense any more. *It was fake,* Jimmy told himself, insisting it over and over to try to drown out the horror of the bombing.

"It was fake!" he murmured through clenched teeth.

"Yes," said his father desperately. "It was! I saw it on TV. It was a fake! I would never have bombed a London tower block. That would make me…"

Only now did Jimmy turn to look at his father. The man's face was pale again and streaked with tears.

"That would make me a monster," he gasped.

21 *TIME TO SHOOT*

The door clicked open before Jimmy could react to his father's words. Mitchell strode in with a TV camera across his shoulder, while Eva struggled in behind him with a long boom microphone, a portable audio mixer strapped over her arm in a protective case, several cables and a couple of sets of headphones.

With a deliberate effort, Jimmy swallowed his emotions. He pulled out the mobile phone from his pocket and handed it to his father.

"Call the Corporation," he ordered.

"What's the number?" Ian Coates asked.

"You're the Prime Minister," Jimmy snarled. "I'm sure you'll remember it."

His father looked shocked for a moment, then quickly nodded and started dialling.

"You want the news desk," Jimmy went on. "You're about to address the nation and they're to broadcast it live, on every channel – just like they did for Miss Bennett."

"The Prime Minister doesn't just call the news desk, Jimmy." Ian Coates held the phone up to his ear, but at the last minute Jimmy grabbed his father's wrist and pressed a button on the handset.

"Speakerphone," he explained. "Just so we all know what's going on."

Coates nodded slowly and held the phone in front of his mouth. When somebody answered, it obviously wasn't the main Corporation switchboard that the general public might have called.

"Specify path," said a man's voice, in an almost robotic tone.

"Cobra, Robin, Alpha, One, Grey," said Ian Coates. His eyes darted across the faces of Jimmy, Mitchell and Eva. They were standing round his bed, staring at him.

There was a click on the other end of the line, then another man's voice came on.

"Hello?" he said. "Prime Minister?"

"Yes," said Coates. "Is that the duty controller?"

"It is, sir." The man sounded uncertain and surprised – as if he'd just been woken up.

"It's good to know these protocols work when we need them, isn't it?" Ian Coates let out a forced laugh. To Jimmy it only made him sound more uneasy.

"Get on with it," Jimmy whispered. "Tell him you need to broadcast a message."

"It looks like I'm going to be addressing the nation,"

said Ian Coates into the phone, his eyes fixed on Jimmy. "I'll need you to broadcast it."

"Addressing the nation?" said the Controller. "Right... OK... Do you need me to send a—"

"I think we have everything we need," Coates interrupted, looking at all of the equipment Mitchell and Eva had brought up. "We have a camera, and I assume that will send the footage to the news van it came from, is that right?"

"Yes, yes..." replied the controller hurriedly. "It'll have an automatic radio link-up, then the feed will be sent by satellite to Corporation House."

"Tell him he has to put it on every channel," Jimmy insisted. "Live."

His father put his thumb over the speaker on the phone and glared at Jimmy.

"You can't force me to do this," he whispered, anger growing in his face. "I'm still in power and I'll be the one to decide—"

"This is the only thing you can do," Jimmy cut in. "The public has to see you've recovered so Miss Bennett can't have you killed and blame it on an illness. And you have to get people back on your side."

"I can't do that with a stupid speech on television!"

"That depends on what you say, doesn't it?"

"I'll say what I like."

"No." Jimmy couldn't help raising his voice, not caring if the duty controller heard him. "There's only one thing

236

you can say to save yourself, and save this country, and I'm going to tell you what it is."

Jimmy and his father stared at each other, but Jimmy could see his father's mind racing through the possibilities. Did he know what he was going to have to do? Did he have any idea how unstable the country was at that moment?

"Put me on every channel," the Prime Minister said at last, into the phone. "Live."

They all waited for a response, but the duty controller said nothing for several seconds. "Is there a problem?" asked Ian Coates.

"Well..." said the voice on the phone.

"Do you need another authorisation code?"

"No... no..." stammered the controller. "We know it's you. You've given the codes, and we have voice recognition software..."

"So what's the problem?" Coates barked.

"I have instructions, sir," the man explained.

"Instructions?"

Jimmy was getting more and more agitated. "Sort this out," he hissed. "We don't have time. Miss Bennett could be sending more..."

"It's instructions from your own Secret Service, sir," said the controller on the phone. "They told me it was an emergency security procedure. Everything is being monitored tonight. I can only put out what comes through their office."

"I'm the Prime Minister!" yelled Coates. "Their office is *my* office!"

"I'm sorry, sir." The man sounded genuinely scared now. "I'm acting on specific orders from Miss Bennett. She was very... persuasive."

Jimmy clenched his fists in annoyance.

"I knew she'd do this," gasped Eva. She turned to Jimmy and whispered, "The Corporation has always been monitored by NJ7 anyway. Now Miss Bennett's taken complete control."

"She can't!" Jimmy cried.

"She can do anything she wants," Eva replied.

"Any more bright ideas?" Ian Coates asked, still clutching the phone. "Can I end this ridiculous call now? I think I'm strong enough to get out of here."

"And go where?" Eva snapped. "If Miss Bennett has control of the Corporation she has control of the whole country whether you're alive or not."

"She's right," Jimmy agreed. "Miss Bennett doesn't even need to kill you if she has power over what people think..." He wanted to say more, but his voice faded away. His head was reeling. There had to be a way to get the Prime Minister on to TV. This was Jimmy's chance to send out a message to the whole country in a way that would force them to listen.

Jimmy could feel his programming attacking his brain from every angle, then his chest convulsed with a powerful surge of energy that burst up from his stomach. His hands leapt to his throat and he felt like he desperately needed to cough, but couldn't. In the corner of his eye, he could just make out Mitchell in exactly the same pose as him – hands clasped around his throat, rocking from side to side, his mouth open, hoping to cough. What was happening?

At last, Jimmy realised. It was obvious. He grabbed for the phone in his father's hand in one sharp movement. At the same time, Mitchell reached out as well. Both of them grasped the handset, their fingers interlocking. They looked up at each other, startled. But before Jimmy could react, the burning in his throat intensified. His lips went soft. He watched the same thing happen to Mitchell, as if he was looking into a mirror.

"Do exactly as I tell you," said Jimmy and Mitchell at precisely the same moment, but their voices weren't their own. Both had produced a perfect imitation of Miss Bennett. They stared at each other. Jimmy could feel his heart pounding so hard he felt like he was being punched.

"Hello?" said the voice on the other end of the line. "Who is that?"

Jimmy drew in a deep breath. His programming was still pumping through him. *Relax*, he ordered himself, but it took his strongest effort to force his fingers to release the phone. He closed his eyes and staggered backwards until he was leaning against the window.

Mitchell's arm snapped up automatically, bringing the phone to his lips. Jimmy mouthed the words with him as he spoke. His muscles seemed to know exactly what the other boy was going to say, before either of them had any idea themselves. And again, it was the voice of Miss Bennett that filled the room.

"This is Miss Bennett," snapped Mitchell. "Since when did it become fashionable to disobey direct orders from your Prime Minister?"

"Miss Bennett?" gasped the duty controller. "You're there?"

"Of course," snapped Mitchell. "I don't let my voice go out unaccompanied."

Jimmy was exhilarated. Mitchell was doing better than he ever could have done himself. Spending so much time with the woman meant Mitchell perfectly replicated not just her voice, but her tone and patterns of speech.

"But you said..." burbled the man on the other end of the phone.

"I know what I said," Mitchell cut in. "I didn't realise I was speaking to a dullard."

"But—"

"Just do as the PM tells you," Mitchell ordered, with a withering sigh.

Only now could Jimmy bring himself to open his eyes. The shock and fear on Mitchell's face was a perfect reflection of his own feelings. It was in total contrast to the authority of the voice coming from Mitchell's throat.

Mitchell handed the phone back to Ian Coates, who obviously knew there was no point resisting Jimmy's instructions. In under a minute, the phone call was over and the Corporation was ready to receive the signal from the hospital. Eva and Jimmy set about the equipment, preparing to film Ian Coates' message to the nation.

It took several seconds before Mitchell was able to help them. He was leaning forwards, supporting himself with one hand on the bed frame, panting hard.

"It was like she was..." he whispered, almost to himself. Jimmy put down the camera and crept up to the other boy.

"Like she was in your throat," he said softly. "But not just your throat. All through your brain as well. Like every memory you've ever had was infected with her. Her voice."

Mitchell turned his head slowly to look at Jimmy out of the corner of his eye. His back straightened, emphasising the power in his shoulders. Even since the last time Jimmy had seen him, Mitchell had grown taller and broader. He nodded once, his bloodshot eyes penetrating Jimmy's skull.

"We're still enemies," he growled. It sent a shiver through Jimmy's frame.

"Come on," said Eva suddenly, shocking Jimmy and Mitchell out of their silent battle. "We're ready. Let's shoot."

Jimmy hurried to pick up the camera, while Eva took control of the sound and Mitchell slunk out of the way of the shot. Ian Coates was busy slicking down his hair and pinching his cheeks to give his face a healthier colour.

"Do you have any make-up, Eva?" he asked. Jimmy

couldn't believe his father was saying that without even a hint of humour. Eva shook her head without looking up from her controls.

"Any idea how to work this?" she said quickly.

"Sorry," said Jimmy, struggling to position the camera comfortably on his shoulder. "It can't be that hard. TV people do it all the time. But don't we need someone in the van?"

"I think it was set up to transmit automatically," Eva explained.

"You think?"

Eva shrugged and looked across at Mitchell, who nodded. Jimmy knew that would have to do.

"OK," he said with a sigh. "You ready?"

Eva nodded. "When we're done you should call that man at the Corporation again and tell him to show more cookery programmes."

Jimmy couldn't help smiling. They both knew Felix was almost addicted to cookery shows and there were never enough of them. Jimmy could feel the warmth of Eva's affection, even though he knew she was nervous and didn't want to reveal to Mitchell or the Prime Minister that she'd been on Jimmy's side all along.

"And more kung-fu movies," Mitchell chipped in. Jimmy was taken aback to see a small smile creeping on to his enemy's face. He almost brought himself to smile back. Finally, Mitchell stepped towards him and planted his huge fists on the camera.

242

"You look like you're having trouble with that," he said quietly, taking the camera from Jimmy and hoisting it on to his own shoulders. Jimmy let it go silently. He could imagine the confusion raging inside Mitchell.

"How do I look?" asked Ian Coates.

Jimmy didn't want to answer. In truth, his father had managed to make himself look much healthier than he was. He even stuck his chest out with an air of authority. But Jimmy wasn't proud of what he saw. Seeing his father taking charge only served as a reminder of the lies he'd told, and how easily he'd abandoned Jimmy. *He's not my real father*, Jimmy repeated over and over to himself, almost trying to turn the man in front of him into an object. Just another obstacle to force out of the way.

"OK," announced Coates, "I think I know what I'm going to say. Let's go."

"No," Jimmy replied quietly. "I'll tell you what to say."

Ian Coates almost choked on his own indignation. Jimmy ignored him. Quickly, he nodded to Mitchell, who aimed the camera at Ian Coates and shifted his hands into position. A small red light came on, on top of the camera. Jimmy picked up his mobile phone and found the TV function.

"You're on," Jimmy announced, a buzz rippling through him. On the tiny screen in his palm was a crystal clear picture of Ian Coates sitting up in his hospital bed.

"Good evening, everybody," Jimmy whispered, suddenly terrified that his father wouldn't say what he was told – either through stubbornness or fear. "Go on!" Jimmy scowled at his father. Now he was convinced this idea was never going to work. But then Ian Coates turned to the camera, his lips curling into an uneasy smile. He took a deep breath, as if, instead of a camera, he was looking into the jaws of a ravenous tiger and any sudden movement would get him devoured. Finally, very slowly, he said, "Good evening, everybody."

22 POWER AND RESPONSIBILITY

Jimmy heard the thoughts charging through his head at a rate of thousands per second. This was his chance. But how much control did he really have over his father? Or, more importantly, how much power did he have over the Prime Minister?

Jimmy wished he knew how to hypnotise people, or trick them into obeying his every word, but instead he just had to trust that his father knew what the consequences would be if he disobeyed. Jimmy had stopped short of harming the man once, but neither of them could predict what his programming would force him to do next time. Then there was the real threat – Miss Bennett. She was out there, somewhere in London, plotting to take power. And this message was the only way to stop her. Jimmy and his father both knew that. Ian Coates had to trust that Jimmy knew what this message had to say to command the attention of the whole country and seize back control. After all, Jimmy had been the one out in the streets, among Londoners, while Ian Coates had been semi-conscious in a hospital bed.

"There have been some shocking accusations made," Jimmy began, as quietly as he could. His father obediently repeated the words, but he sounded awkward. "So I have decided to put an end to all the rumours." Again, Ian Coates copied Jimmy word for word. He was gradually beginning to sound more fluent, as if he was inventing the speech himself.

"I am alive and well," Jimmy went on, with his father repeating everything perfectly. "And I am still in charge of Great Britain." Now Ian Coates started embellishing Jimmy's speech, adding that he was, "proud to be at the helm of a great nation". Jimmy didn't mind. If it made the speech sound more adult, it would have a stronger effect.

"And I didn't blow up that tower block," said Jimmy.

"The horrors that have been laid at my door," said his father, "are groundless lies put about by our French enemy simply to weaken our national resolve."

No, thought Jimmy, *stick to what I tell you!* He could feel his control slipping, but had to carry on.

"There is no need for war," said Jimmy. He paused, waiting for his father.

Eventually, Ian Coates said it: "There is no need for war."

"And I ask the French to agree to settle our differences peacefully."

"And I call on the French nation," said the Prime Minister, "to join me in exploring a peaceful resolution to our differences." Jimmy clenched his jaw, growing nervous about his father's changes to his speech.

"What the country needs now," said Jimmy firmly.

"What the country needs now..."

"And the only right way to run Britain," Jimmy went on.

"And the only right way to run Britain..." Ian Coates slowed nervously.

"...is for people to vote." Jimmy spat the words viciously, as if he could stab each one on to his father's tongue so he could never shake them off. But his father was silent.

"Say it," insisted Jimmy. "The only right way to run Britain is for people to vote." All he could hear was his heart thudding hard inside him. How could he force his father to call a democratic general election? It would change everything. And it would also go against everything Ian Coates believed in.

The silence stretched out so long Jimmy could feel his muscles trembling, preparing for action. But he knew there was no fight that could help him now. It was words that would win this battle. But then Jimmy felt his muscles trembling harder, almost violently. Something inside him had realised that he wasn't completely powerless.

Jimmy's throat erupted with a flaming sensation. The breath caught in his chest and his mouth seemed to swirl with every fear and every joy he had ever known. His lips parted and he knew what sound was going to come out.

"What the country needs now," he said, his words booming around the room. It was easily loud enough to be picked up by the microphone in Eva's hand, and it was the voice of his father. "The only right way to run Britain is..."

"...is for people to vote." It was the real Ian Coates that finished the sentence. He said it quickly, like he was spitting out a sour sweet. Jimmy coughed and spluttered, but he managed to force out the next words, again in his father's voice.

"A democratic gener..."

"General election." Again, the real Ian Coates completed the phrase carefully articulating every syllable in a breathless, flat tone. Jimmy watched, aghast. His father ran a trembling hand through his hair, then pulled in a deep breath and puffed his chest out even further. "I'm calling a democratic general election," he repeated. This time his voice was firm and smooth. Along with his voice, his body was changing too. His muscles relaxed. Within a few seconds he looked stronger – commanding.

"You will have the chance to vote for who you want to be the leader of this country," he said, without waiting for any prompting from Jimmy. He didn't need it. Now he knew what Jimmy had been planning. And he'd gone along with it. "The era of these monstrous attacks on Britain must be brought to an end. We must unite our great nation once more." Jimmy couldn't believe what he was seeing – and hearing. His father, Ian Coates, the leader of the Neo-democratic state of Great Britain, was ending Neo-democracy and calling for a free vote. An election. Jimmy's whole body was hot with excitement.

At the same time, his father was transforming from an invalid pretending to be strong, to a man with power coursing through him. It was as if the man had been taken over by inner powers of his own – those of a politician. "To do that," he went on, "I'm calling a general election." He leaned forward slightly, then jabbed two weak fists at the camera. "And I intend to win it."

The final, smug grin that Ian Coates gave the camera made Jimmy want to throw up. He watched the screen on his phone fade to black, then looked up to see Mitchell putting the camera down. Only now did the words of his father's speech sink in.

"You've done it," Jimmy whispered. "You've ended Neo-democracy."

Ian Coates stared blankly across the room. Jimmy didn't care. His speech on TV was enough.

"You *will* have an election?" Jimmy asked, buzzing with triumph, but nervous about celebrating prematurely.

His father nodded, scowling. "I have to now," he said. "People will expect it. If I look like I'm changing my mind after what I just said, I'll lose all authority. So yes, there'll be an election. But as soon as I've won—"

"You won't win," Jimmy insisted. "People won't—"

"People will do what they're told." Ian Coates paused, then added, "If they're told in the right way."

Jimmy opened his mouth to argue, but something sent a ripple through his muscles. A noise. He looked across at the others and realised that only Mitchell had heard it too.

"They're outside," said Mitchell. "They're coming in."

"Quick," said Jimmy to his father. "If you're feeling stronger, we can get you out into the corridor. Then we'll find a different room and lure Miss Bennett's men in here. We'll—"

"There's no need for that now, Jimmy," said Ian Coates calmly.

"Come on!" Jimmy insisted. "We've got to move!" His father stayed put, and when Jimmy looked across at Mitchell and Eva, they weren't moving either.

"Jimmy," said Eva gently. "He's shown the country he's alive and that he's in charge. They can't kill him now. Miss Bennett would never be able to take power without everybody knowing what she'd done."

"She's a killer, Jimmy," added Ian Coates, "but only in secret. Her secrets are her strength."

"Your plan worked," Mitchell insisted. "You put Mr Coates on TV so that Miss Bennett couldn't try to take over."

"So why are they...?" Jimmy's words dried up when he saw the eyes of Eva, Mitchell and the Prime Minister all boring into him.

"They're here for you, Jimmy," announced Ian Coates, with no emotion.

"Me?" Jimmy's throat was so dry his voice hardly registered.

"I expect you made quite a scene on your way in," said the PM. "Did you think that would go unnoticed? Or that the agents you knocked out wouldn't come round eventually? I'm surprised it took them this long."

Jimmy heard the lift shaft bringing NJ7 closer and the pounding of feet on the stairs. His hearing heightened every sound in the building, and his muscles seemed to reach out, probing for vibrations.

"Then there was the broadcast," Ian Coates continued. "The general public might not have realised what was happening, but Miss Bennett would have known straight away. She probably had her technicians enhance the sound of your whisper." He hesitated to clear his throat. "No, I'm sure of it. That's her NJ7 reinforcements. And they're here for you."

Everything inside Jimmy was driving him to move. *Escape* he heard in his head. *Survive! Move NOW!* But he fought his own limbs and forced all his energy to work against that potent voice rooted deep inside him. He wanted to stay. He wanted answers.

"Why would they..." he began, but couldn't finish. He stared into his father's face and could feel the heat rising inside him. "You're in charge again," he insisted. "You can tell them..."

Ian Coates' expression made Jimmy's words meaningless. The man was trying to look calm, but to

Jimmy the fear in his eyes was obvious. From the corridor came the sound of the lift doors opening.

"You can't do this," Jimmy begged. "Give them new orders! You're my father!"

From the corridor came the sound of scuffling feet. Were they searching the rooms? How long did Jimmy have? He could feel his programming charging his muscles.

"I care about you Jimmy," replied Ian Coates. Jimmy's senses were too overwhelmed to work out whether it sounded true. "But even if I was your biological father, I'd still be the Prime Minister. I have responsibilities."

"I don't understand!" Jimmy protested. "Why is it your responsibility to kill me?"

"You're a threat."

"To who?"

"To everything the country stands for!"

"That's not true!" Jimmy screamed it, not caring if it gave away his position. "I saved you!"

"But you're still my enemy!" his father bellowed back. "How many times have you refused to work for this Government? How many times have you deliberately sabotaged British operations? And now that there's going to be an election, you're going to fight for Christopher Viggo, aren't you?" The man was smouldering with rage. His eyes were bloodshot and his hands trembled. "So don't you question what my responsibilities are!"

Ian Coates at last tore his gaze from Jimmy. He turned to Mitchell and hissed, "Your country needs you."

Zafi's phone vibrated in her pocket. She pulled it out with a huff of annoyance as she slipped her way through the crowds. Even as she read the message, she kept up her pace, snaking across London on foot.

In an instant, the string of letters and numbers on her phone danced into new positions, twisting in her head to reveal the message. It was another update from her bosses at the DGSE. They'd just intercepted a broadcast from Ian Coates on Corporation TV and they advised Zafi to check the hospitals to complete the assassination.

Zafi snorted a dry laugh. She was already sprinting across Westminster Bridge, towards St Thomas'.

Jimmy's world swam. He couldn't shout. He couldn't even think. The effect of Ian Coates' words was ferocious. It was the stab of betrayal in a wound that was already gaping. And it was the crumbling of every emotional defence he thought he had built up against his father. Every organ in his body seemed to turn to ash.

Meanwhile, Mitchell responded as if a bolt of electricity had been shot through him. He stood upright and every muscle tensed.

"Mitchell!" gasped Eva, but she held herself back.

Was it from shock or because she still needed to appear loyal to the Prime Minister?

Jimmy realised Mitchell was hesitating. *That's the only reason I'm still alive*, he heard himself thinking. He could feel the weakness growing inside him, latching on to his emotions and spreading through his entire body. Tears came to his eyes. *No!* Jimmy forced himself to search for his inner assassin. It had no emotions. It had no weakness. *Crush this pain!* Jimmy begged his own body.

Then Mitchell's face contorted into a stern grimace. His lips opened like a crack in a rock and his voice came out in a coarse rumble: "I obey orders."

In a move so fast, Jimmy didn't even see it begin, Mitchell scooped up the TV camera from the floor and hurled the whole thing across the room. It came like a giant bullet. Jimmy couldn't duck in time. He was only just able to shield his head with his arms. The camera sent him flying to the floor with the force of a traffic accident.

The sound of Eva's scream jolted Jimmy's muscles to the next gear. He rolled across the lino just in time to avoid a body slam from Mitchell. At the end of his second roll, Jimmy's hands landed perfectly on the shaft of the boom mic. In one smooth sweep, Jimmy slammed the big fuzzy end into Mitchell's midriff and used the force of the impact to push himself to his feet.

Before he even knew what his body was planning, Jimmy sprinted towards the window, still holding the boom mic. At the last instant, he leapt into the air. *I'm going to die*, he thought, but his programming punched through his brain and pounded his fear to dust.

Jimmy led with his feet, slamming them into the middle of the glass. At the same moment, he trailed the boom mic behind him, and without even looking back he used the end of the pole to scoop the sheets from his father's bed. Glass exploded into his face. Then he hit the cold air and plummeted towards the ground.

23 BURYING A HATCHET

Jimmy felt his body hurtling downwards. Blood rushed to his face. He even tasted some in his mouth. He couldn't believe he was plummeting from the same hospital for a second time in twenty-four hours. But once again his programming was in control. His arms swirled the boom mic in a huge circle above his head. The hospital bed sheet whirled round like a sail caught on the blade of a windmill.

Jimmy pumped harder and harder. His shoulders were burning. The air still rushed past, and the shadows of the ground loomed upwards. But the effect of the swirling sheet was half-parachute, half-helicopter. It was never going to be as effective as either of those would have been, but it did something. Then Jimmy's mind threw up one image that his programming had locked away in his memory – the trees lining the river outside the hospital.

Jimmy crunched through the branches then hit the pavement feet first. His legs crumpled and he landed cruelly on his hip, then his shoulder slammed into the stone. The impact jarred his whole body, thrusting an involuntary cry from his chest. For a second he lay on the pavement, seeing the world in a sideways blur. In his weakness, a crazy idea flashed across his mind: maybe he'd landed so hard his powers had been smacked out of him. Maybe he could just lie there and let pain take him over – normal, wonderful pain.

Get up, he heard in his head, crashing through his fantasy. He dropped the boom rod and wiped his mouth with the back of his hand. It came away smeared with blood. Jimmy didn't have time to care. He staggered to his feet, but he could barely stand and his left leg was numb. He glanced up. Was Mitchell following him? The bed sheet was stretched out in the branches, obscuring the view.

Jimmy tried to run, but after two hobbled steps he half-collapsed and had to support himself with a hand along the low wall. This wasn't going to work, even though he could already feel the thrumming of his programming sending relief to the bones in his leg.

The answer was obvious. The speedboat he'd used as a ramp was still there – overturned on the wall a few metres away. Without hesitating, Jimmy vaulted over the wall and threw himself into one of the other boats. The roar of the motor sent a shiver of exhilaration through his muscles. The Thames sprayed around him, a huge arch on either side. He swung the boat into the centre of the river, cranking it up to full power.

Still wincing from the pain through his whole body, and tilting heavily to one side, Jimmy roared forwards. On his right was the hospital; on his left were the Houses of Parliament. Jimmy ripped towards Westminster Bridge, splitting London in two.

Eva let out one piercing scream, then pulled herself together. Mitchell and Jimmy had whirled around each other in the centre of the room so quickly they almost melted into one. Then came the crashing of the window. Eva instinctively shielded her face and flinched away from the glass. Her view of Jimmy hurtling out of the window was blocked by the flapping of the bed sheets that trailed behind him like a huge flag of surrender.

He's going to die, Eva thought. *He can't survive that fall.* She looked to Mitchell, but he was already climbing out through the broken pane of glass.

"Is he...?" Eva called out. She couldn't finish and Mitchell didn't respond. He simply climbed out and disappeared, without even looking back. Did that mean Jimmy was still alive? Had Mitchell seen him? Eva's head was pounding. Her heart wouldn't stop hammering. It took her a long time to realise that now she was alone with Ian Coates. The Prime Minister was sitting awkwardly on his bed, his paisley pyjamas completely exposed now that his sheets were gone. He was staring vacantly after the two boys.

"Do you think...?" Eva began.

Coates turned to her, but his thoughts were obviously far away. Flashes of confusion and anger alternated on his face. He was about to speak, when the door burst open.

"What was that?" It was Miss Bennett.

"You!" gasped Coates. He swung his legs round and tried to stand, but it took more effort than he'd expected and he ended up perched on the edge of the bed.

Miss Bennett marched straight over to the window. Three men followed her in, all of them built like upturned mountains. They had earpieces and on their lapels were green stripes.

"Send out the word," Miss Bennett muttered. "The target's loose."

Eva felt her heart lurch again. Jimmy was still alive. She didn't know how, but he had to be. Otherwise Miss Bennett's reaction would have been very different.

"Secure the rest of the building just in case," Miss Bennett went on. The three men rushed away. "And check the roof. I heard something."

Finally, Miss Bennett turned to Ian Coates. Even in these extreme circumstances she leaned against the empty window frame with no visible tension in her body. She dipped her head slightly to one side and brushed a hair from her face. Eva was fascinated. With that softness round her eyes and her lips pursed, she looked like she could either kiss you or kill you, Eva thought.

259

"I enjoyed your speech," she said softly.

"I hope it made a better impression than the last speech of mine that ended up on TV."

"People seem satisfied," said Miss Bennett. "They'll be a bit confused, I think – a Neo-democratic Prime Minister calling for a general election. As if you returning from near-death wasn't enough. But..." She shrugged. "The public is always confused. It's better that way. As long as they're not rioting, who cares what they think?"

"We have to care now," Coates insisted. "I've called an election. It was the only way..."

"Don't worry," Miss Bennett purred. "We'll win the election. Who's going to be our opposition? Christopher Viggo? We can handle him."

Eva watched Ian Coates carefully. He was shivering and his eyes were flickering rapidly. "What about William Lee?" he asked. "Is he the one who poisoned me? Was he trying to take power?" His voice rose and fell wildly as he spoke, as if he couldn't control it.

"He was trying to take power," Miss Bennett replied. "But he didn't poison you. I'm fairly confident of that."

Eva couldn't understand what was happening. Ian Coates knew Miss Bennett was the one who had tried to poison him. She and Mitchell had told him themselves. Eva shot a glance at Miss Bennett, who glared back with the power of a precision laser.

"Personally," said Miss Bennett lightly, "when anything goes wrong, I find it best to blame the French."

Suddenly Eva understood. Miss Bennett and Ian Coates both knew the truth. But what good did it do to spill it all out? There was nothing Ian Coates could do to protect himself from Miss Bennett – he couldn't arrest her; he couldn't condemn her. And she had nothing to gain now from harming him.

"The public will like that," Coates agreed. "So what about William Lee?" he added cautiously. "Should I deal with him?"

"No," Miss Bennett replied immediately. "He's been disgraced in public. There's nothing he can do to hurt us now. Nowhere he can go. He certainly can't help Viggo. And he has certain... skills. We'd be fools to waste a good man. He'll serve me."

"He'll serve us," said Coates tentatively.

Miss Bennett shook her head slowly and very slowly whispered, "Me."

Ian Coates dropped his gaze to his lap. Eva could almost feel his spirit collapsing. "What about..." the man mumbled, waving a limp hand towards Eva. "Mitchell too. Do we...?"

Eva's blood froze in an instant. Miss Bennett beamed at her. It was the most frightening smile Eva had ever seen.

"Eva!" Miss Bennett exclaimed, letting out a laugh like dark honey. "Eva and Mitchell have proved their loyalty to the Government this evening, haven't they?"

Eva nodded, unable to look anywhere but straight into Miss Bennett's huge brown eyes.

"So now," Miss Bennett went on, her smile melting into a complete blank, "they must prove their loyalty to me."

Eva froze. It took a huge effort to draw breath into her lungs. Her terror was crippling. "Yes..." she said, her voice sticking in her throat, "...Prime Minister."

"Oh!" Miss Bennett brought her hand to her mouth in shock and laughed again. "Don't go calling me that, Eva," she said. "No – this gentleman here made it quite clear on television this evening who was Prime Minister. Weren't you watching?"

Eva looked from Miss Bennett to Ian Coates to clear up her confusion, but Coates was just sitting on the edge of his bed, his head in his hands.

"I'll never be Prime Minister now," Miss Bennett explained. "But in the last half an hour I realised that I don't need to be. Because the Prime Minister..." She held out a hand in the direction of Jimmy's father. "...He's done enough to show me that it's far better to run the country without anybody knowing who you are. It's much easier to keep secrets that way." She lowered her voice to a whisper and paused between every word. "Secrets. Are. Power."

Suddenly, Ian Coates let out a desperate groan. Eva watched him rock backwards and forwards, holding his head. "Do you need a doctor?" she asked.

Coates replied by throwing his head back and wailing. Eva could see that his face was wet with tears. "What have I done?" he cried.

"Oh, be quiet," Miss Bennett snapped. "You've done nothing. I organised a fire drill in good time to make sure that tower block was evacuated. I wasn't going to let you—"

"But I—"

"You did what you had to do." Miss Bennett's tone was disapproving, almost disgusted. "Powerful men must make difficult decisions."

"Am I a powerful man?" Coates whimpered. "Or am I...?"

"You're not powerful any more," Miss Bennett answered. "So it doesn't matter whether you're evil or not."

"It matters to me!" Coates yelled at the top of his voice. He heaved himself to his feet and staggered across the room towards Miss Bennett and Eva. "The tower block!" he howled. "What could have...?"

"That was William Lee's plan!" Miss Bennett shouted. "You only put it into action because the poison was already in your brain."

"You think I was mad?" Coates cried, saliva hanging from the corner of his mouth. "You're blaming the poison?"

Miss Bennett didn't reply. It was as if she could hardly bear to look at him.

"What about my son!" said Coates, still staggering across the room, tiny step by tiny step. "Was I mad just now when I sent Mitchell to kill him?"

Miss Bennett looked disgusted. "Get back into bed," she ordered. "You did what you had to..."

BOOM!

The end of Miss Bennett's sentence was cut off by a fireball in the corridor. The internal wall was blasted to shreds like tissue paper in a volcano. The rest of the windows shattered. Eva and Miss Bennett were both thrown to the floor. Ian Coates was hurled back on to his bed. Eva couldn't see anything but black smoke. It stung her eyes and seemed to wrap itself around her. She coughed and spluttered – and heard Miss Bennett and Ian Coates doing the same. At least that told her they were all still alive and conscious.

In fact, the explosion had seemed more powerful than it actually was. It had been designed to maximise surprise, to create a huge amount of smoke and to leave the Prime Minister completely exposed to anybody attacking from inside the building.

At last a clearing opened up in the billows of blackness. Eva waved the smoke away with one hand, covering her mouth and nose with the other. Before she could see what was happening, there was a flash and the crack of a gun. Then came another shot. That's when Eva caught a glimpse of Ian Coates, curled up under his bed. Miss Bennett was standing next to the bed, shouting into a mobile phone held in the crook of her neck. Eva couldn't hear what she was saying because her ears were ringing from the explosion and the gunshots.

Miss Bennett was holding her gun out in front of her,

cradled in both hands. She trained it from side to side and fired into the darkness again, towards the lift shaft. Eva couldn't help flinching at the sounds of the shots. Who was out there?

When the attacker finally appeared, it took Eva several seconds to believe what she was seeing. It looked as if the smoke itself was attacking. A streak of black flew towards Miss Bennett at chest level. It knocked the gun from her hands and sent her mobile phone clattering across the floor. The strike looked effortless – like a tornado snatching a balloon from a baby.

Miss Bennett just managed to stay on her feet, but now she was confronted by a short, slim figure dressed head to toe in black. Only the gleam of the eyes revealed that this was a human being. Although, if Eva had been able to see through the mask, she would have known that this being was only 38 per cent human. From NJ7 files, she would have recognised the face of the French Secret Service's most powerful and sophisticated weapon – Zafi Sauvage.

24 THE LAIR OF THE RIVER SPIDER

Miss Bennett dropped her bodyweight to the left and raised her hands to shield her head. Somehow, she managed to retain the elegance Eva was used to seeing in her, but combined it with a new speed – and self-defence techniques from four continents. Nevertheless, she was no match for Zafi.

Zafi spun on the ball of her left foot, slamming her right knee into Miss Bennett's side. There was nothing elegant about Miss Bennett's fall. She sprawled across the lino and ended up barely a metre from Eva, wheezing for air and scrabbling for her phone.

"No!" Ian Coates cried out from his shelter under the bed. Eva read it on the man's lips – she was still slightly deafened. Then she just made out the crackle of Miss Bennett's mobile phone. It was lying on the floor between them. At first, Eva couldn't hear what was being said, but gradually her ears cleared. A single question was being repeated over and over: "One rope or two?"

What did it mean? Eva watched in horror as Zafi flicked the bed away with one hand. It flipped over and almost flew through the empty window frame. Ian Coates was left cowering on the floor.

"Save me!" he yelled, his eyes imploring Miss Bennett to act.

"One rope or two?" came the question again, crackling out of the mobile phone on the floor. Miss Bennett grabbed Eva's ankle. What was happening? Then everything became clear when a helicopter arrived, hovering a short distance from the building, outside the window. The smoke was blown away in huge plumes.

Over the drone of the rotors, Eva heard the high pitched squeal of something streaking through the air. Then a rope flew in through the window, shot from the chopper. It landed right next to Miss Bennett, who snatched it up and wrapped it round her forearm. Almost instantly, the rope retracted. Together, Miss Bennett and Eva were dragged across the floor.

Eva saw Zafi raise her arm above her head, ready to strike. Eva slid across the lino, pulled by Miss Bennett's lock-like grip. She glanced up into Miss Bennett's face. Her lips were parted to speak, but there was a moment of hesitation. The woman's eyes were fixed on Ian Coates.

Finally, Miss Bennett and Eva scrambled to their feet. They had to dive out of the window to avoid slamming into the wall. As Eva was hauled out into the night sky, she heard Miss Bennett let out a mighty cry: "TWO!"

Almost instantaneously, a second rope shot out of the helicopter. Eva felt herself twisting upside-down in mid-air. Miss Bennett had her by the ankle, and it gave her the perfect view of the room she'd just left. She squinted in the wind to see the weight on the end of the rope slam into Ian Coates' back. The assassin's hand swept downwards. Eva couldn't stop herself screaming – partly from the rush of being extracted from the top floor of a building by a rapid flight, partly from the pain of Miss Bennett's nails in her ankle, but mostly from the utter conviction that the Prime Minister's head was about to be cracked open like a coconut.

But Zafi's hand swished through empty air. At the last split-second, Ian Coates' rope retracted – with him desperately clinging to the end. Eva crash landed in the cabin of the helicopter. At once, she twisted on to her front and peered back into the hospital. Ian Coates was flying to join them. How had Zafi missed her chance? She'd had long enough to complete the job, thought Eva.

As Ian Coates scrambled on board and lay panting alongside her, Eva's fear was ebbing away, replaced by a thousand questions. Only one stood out – was it possible that the French assassin suffered from glimmers of the same moral doubts that lived in Jimmy?

There was no time to think about it now. The helicopter banked sharply to the side and soared high into the clouds, heading for the safety of Daws Hill Royal Air Force Station. Eva propped herself up against the wall of the helicopter, while Miss Bennett heaved Ian Coates towards her.

"Congratulations!" she shouted, her hair flying wildly about her face in the wind. "You're still alive and you're still Prime Minister." Her smile vanished and she yanked Coates closer until their noses were almost touching. "Your life is mine," she sneered.

Westminster Bridge was still crowded. As Jimmy hurtled under it, people leaned over the rail to see what was happening. Jimmy was vaguely aware of the line of faces, lit by the ghostly yellow lamplight reflected off the water. There was an "ooh" from the crowd. In less than a second, he left them behind. He tore under the bridge and out the other side in a rainbow cascade of water. He swerved to avoid a huge recycling trawler and twisted in and out between three smaller vessels.

To his right, the pods of the London Eye twinkled. But Jimmy was moving too fast to enjoy the sights. His body was acting in perfect synchrony with the boat, the slightest twitch in his forearms adjusting the weight distribution. Then, over the roar of the boat's motor, Jimmy's ears picked up a second 'ooh'. He didn't need to look round. He knew straight away that another boat was close behind him, and he knew exactly who must be driving it.

In fact, it wasn't just one boat. Behind him, Mitchell stood astride two speedboats, powering them forwards side by side, one foot inside each. Just as he came out from under Westminster Bridge, he twisted the wheel of the right hand boat and ripped it off with one massive tug. It locked the steering. Then he stamped his foot down to unbalance the whole boat and kicked it away. He jumped with both feet into the left-hand boat and rapidly steered that way.

The two boats curved round on either side of the recycling trawler then headed back towards the centre of the river. The two symmetrical arcs were leading them into a collision – but Mitchell had calculated the two courses perfectly. At the point of impact, they would crush Jimmy's boat between them.

Weaving round the obstacles in the centre of the river had slowed Jimmy down just enough for Mitchell's two boats to catch him. They were bending towards him in a vicious pincer. He couldn't accelerate any harder, but if he slowed down or stopped Mitchell would merely adjust his course to cut him off sooner. There was only one option.

Jimmy's eyes scanned the bridge ahead of him – Hungerford Bridge. Really it was three bridges in one – two footbridges on either side of a central railway line. Even sooner than Jimmy expected, Mitchell's boats loomed towards him. Their tips attacked like black sabres, ready to skewer whatever came between them. As soon as Jimmy hit the shadow of Hungerford Bridge, he took a two step run-up, mounting the bow of the speedboat, and leapt into the air.

In his peripheral vision, he just caught sight of Mitchell making the same jump. That instant, all three boats smashed together. One was thrown directly upwards. The other two exploded on impact. The ball of flame ignited the boat that was already in mid-air, causing a double-blast more spectacular than any firework display. There was another "ooh" from Westminster Bridge.

The crowd may have had the perfect view of the destruction of the boats, but Jimmy was out of sight now, hanging from the structural beams under Hungerford Bridge. Only a faint light reflected off the water. Jimmy's night vision purred in his head and he knew Mitchell's would be doing the same. The shadows were still deep and the corners between the struts created cavernous hiding places. It was like a metal spider web in three dimensions. But was Jimmy the spider, or the trapped fly?

At first Jimmy thought about dropping into the water and trying to swim away, but he knew that would immediately betray his position, and Mitchell was just as strong a swimmer. Better to finish it now. And Jimmy knew from experience that his best chance was to give Mitchell something to think about.

"You heard what the Prime Minister said," Jimmy called out, constantly shifting to obscure his position, clambering around the bridge like a giant insect. His words echoed round the metal and bounced off the water. "There's going to be an election." There was no reply. A pigeon hooted and flapped away.

Jimmy swung quickly between the struts, each of them turned a hazy blue by his night vision. His grip was slippery and he kept moving through huge cobwebs. He had to wipe his face and spit the dust from his lips. He pulled his feet up to take some of the weight and to make himself as invisible as possible. There was no sign of Mitchell.

Perhaps he'd already gone, Jimmy thought. Maybe he was trying to call in support from other NJ7 agents. Jimmy dismissed that idea immediately. It was strange that NJ7 hadn't sent anybody else by now, but whatever the reason for that, Jimmy knew Mitchell wasn't going anywhere.

Of course, if Jimmy had known that every other NJ7 agent in the area was trying to deal with Zafi, it might have given him some confidence. As it was, all he could feel was the throb of his inner assassin, and a grave sense of dread. He had to lure Mitchell into the open.

"An election changes everything!" Jimmy shouted. "You know that, don't you? "Neo-democracy is over." Still, Mitchell didn't respond. *He's learned*, Jimmy realised. *He's adapted*. Then a question flashed through his mind: *Why haven't I?*

"In a few weeks," Jimmy called out, his voice wavering, "people will vote and the Government that sent you to kill me will be nothing."

At last Mitchell broke his silence. "I don't think I want to hang around here that long," came the shout.

Jimmy's brain fizzed as if an electric current had been switched on. His programming created a picture of the sound of Mitchell's voice, trying to pinpoint his position.

"I'm voting now," Mitchell went on. "I vote that I kill you." And that's when he struck.

25 MESSAGE SENT

A whoosh behind Jimmy alerted him just in time. His reaction was so fast he didn't even know what he was doing until he'd done it. Mitchell was hanging from a metal girder directly behind Jimmy and his foot was flying towards Jimmy's neck.

Jimmy squeezed a strut between his feet and let go with his hands. His upper body dropped. Mitchell's trainer swished past Jimmy's face so close he felt the rubber on the end of his nose. Jimmy swung upside-down, but crunched his stomach muscles to bring his shoulders up again immediately. He relaxed his legs to let his lower half drop, leaving him in mid-air for a split second. Straightaway he caught that same strut with the tips of his fingers and kicked out behind him. He connected perfectly with one foot on each half of Mitchell's ribcage.

The two boys swung round each other like Olympic gymnasts on monkey bars. They traded blows with such pace that the noise of each strike echoed into the next. It sounded like rapid drumming. Jimmy let his mind drown completely in his programming. He wheeled his legs round, throwing himself in complete rotations to spin and kick again. At the same time he blocked Mitchell's attacks with alternate hands – while his right defended against a savage kick, his left held on to the strut above his head, then vice versa.

Eventually, actions merged together. The fight became a blur in Jimmy's head. He felt like he was in a trance, with a red haze seeping from his centre out towards the tips of his limbs. It was the feeling of murder. He knew Mitchell felt it too, and the longer the fight went on the hotter it burned.

One of us is going to die, Jimmy heard himself thinking. *I can't stop it.* Even as he twisted and landed a kick in Mitchell's stomach, he wanted to cry out, as if he could wake himself from his daze. Except that it wasn't a daze – it was his programming and it was stronger than ever.

With the flickering light from the water and his night vision, what Jimmy saw started to distort. First he couldn't tell the difference between Mitchell's fists and his own. Mitchell's legs blended into his legs. For a horrifying flash, he thought he saw his own features on Mitchell's face.

No, Jimmy thought, desperately trying to break into his own consciousness. He forced himself to look away.

His body followed and he swung across the width of the bridge to the very edge, until he could reach up and hook his fingers on to the walkway. Mitchell followed like a deadly shadow. When Jimmy looked again at his opponent, the light had shifted again. The tricks in Jimmy's brain projected an older face on to Mitchell's body: the face of Ian Coates.

"NO!" Jimmy screamed. He closed his eyes and pushed a lifetime of fury into one final kick. For once, Mitchell's defence was insufficient. Jimmy's foot crashed into the other boy's chin. Mitchell's head rocked back and a fountain of blood spurted from his nose. *Finish it*, Jimmy heard his programming growl.

Jimmy fought against his own arms, forbidding them to strike out while Mitchell was unguarded. A single punch at the base of his neck would send Mitchell's dead body dropping into the Thames. Jimmy deliberately squeezed his fingers into the metal, as if he could send down roots that would hold them in place. Then they started vibrating.

At first Jimmy thought his body was resisting his will, but then he heard a sound that made sense of everything: the clatter of a train. Jimmy was hanging from the first of the three bridges that ran alongside each other: a footbridge. But barely a metre behind his head was the central passage: the railway bridge.

Just then, Mitchell shook off Jimmy's strike and launched his counter-attack. But Jimmy was already swinging to gather momentum. Then he threw himself backwards. The last thing he saw was the wide red streak that ran from Mitchell's nose, completely covering the grimace on his lips.

Jimmy flipped over and pulled his knees into his chest. He judged the thrust of his flight perfectly. He had enough distance to reach the railway line and enough height to curl over the safety fence. He landed on his feet, but couldn't keep his balance and immediately fell backwards, tripping on the railway line. He landed with his neck on one rail, staring straight down the track towards the oncoming train. The tremors in the cold steel seemed to stir up Jimmy's resolve. He didn't have time to be afraid and simply rolled across the track to the other side. The train rattled past a split-second later.

Jimmy knew Mitchell wouldn't give up. Perhaps he had already followed Jimmy on to the railway bridge. But before there was any chance of the fight continuing, Jimmy jumped up and caught the side of one of the carriages. He closed his eyes and rested his head against the metal, breathing slowly and deeply, regardless of the thick diesel fumes.

In his mind, the hammering of the train became Mitchell howling for him in the night, and merged with his own silent screams.

In a tiny cell at Westminster police station, William Lee's

huge frame looked wildly out of place. He leaned back in his chair, staring up at the ceiling and listening to the creaking of the metal legs. In his head, he replayed the events of the last few hours, trying to work out logically where things had gone wrong and formulating a plan for what he should do next.

As soon as he'd seen that Miss Bennett had that recording of him, he knew that she was going to manipulate the media to further her own power. What he hadn't been prepared for was how quickly she'd been able to do it. Lee felt a crushing shame in his heart at the memory of seeing himself ranting on TV. He'd immediately changed his plan. Instead of taking over the country, he'd realised he needed to get as far away as possible. He'd reached the end of Downing Street before Miss Bennett's men picked him up.

A part of him wanted to admit that Miss Bennett had acted masterfully, but he couldn't detach his emotions. Suddenly, he jumped to his feet, snatched up the chair by one leg and slammed it against the wall over and over. He only stopped when he heard the clang of the door behind him.

Lee dropped the misshapen lump of metal and plastic, drew himself up to his full height and smoothed back the hair on the sides of his head.

"What is it?" he snarled.

There was no reply, and Lee turned to see one of the NJ7 agents who had brought him in leaning casually in the doorway. He beckoned with his head for Lee to follow and together they marched along the cells and back up the stairs to the offices.

A duty officer was waiting with Lee's personal belongings in a clear plastic bag – including his watch, his wallet and phone – even his tie, belt and shoes. One by one each item was handed back to him and ticked off a list.

"What's happening?" Lee asked, still maintaining that air of authority in his voice.

"There was an attack on the Prime Minister," replied the agent. "And Miss Bennett. She wants you released."

"So the attack failed?"

"Unfortunately for you – yes."

Lee rushed to tie his shoelaces, but tried to disguise his eagerness to get out of the police station. "So Coates wants me back," he said proudly.

"Not Coates," the agent explained. "Miss Bennett."

Lee dropped his laces and snapped bolt upright. He was at least a head taller than the NJ7 agent and stared down at the man. "I don't want to," Lee announced flatly. "Take me back to my cell."

"I don't think you have a choice," replied the agent, not making eye contact.

Lee took a long time to think. Eventually he picked up his tie and started threading it round his neck. "What happened?" he asked. He had to get as much information as he could from this agent before he was thrown into the lion's den.

"Nothing serious," the agent replied, peering through the blind at the dark street. "They've had routine medical checks. I hear Miss Bennett and the Prime Minister are being treated for minor burns. Nothing more. There was a small explosion at the hospital." He paused and stroked his chin as if he was considering what might have happened. "Oh, and that girl was with them too."

"Girl?" said Lee. "You mean Eva?"

"That's the one. She got burned too. Also not serious. You're to report to her at 0700."

"Report to *Eva*?" Lee snatched his wallet from the duty officer and shoved it roughly into his jacket pocket. "Surely you mean I should report to Miss Bennett."

The agent shook his head. "Eva Doren," he confirmed, still refusing to look directly at Lee. "She'll brief you in the morning. You work for her."

The agent turned away and Lee was sure he did it to hide his smirk. The agent signed a piece of paper on the duty officer's desk and led Lee out of the building.

"Get in the car," he ordered, pointing to the waiting NJ7 vehicle.

Lee refused to budge. "You address your seniors as 'sir'," he growled.

The agent calmly climbed into the driver's seat, started the engine and rolled down the window. Now, for the first time, he fixed Lee with a cold stare. "Get in the car," he said.

Lee felt the chill of the air bite through to his core. He

strode forwards and folded into the back seat, having to pull his knees almost up to his chest to fit in.

Neither man said another word to each other. Lee let the streets of Central London blur outside the window before closing his eyes and pinching the top of his nose to fight back the extreme tiredness. He felt a sickness in his stomach and his mind was churning. After a minute he pulled out his phone and clutched it in his palm. There were several messages waiting for him, but he ignored them. His thoughts were somewhere else.

Moving slowly at first, then faster and faster, he ran his thumb over the buttons, typing a text message. When he was finished, he reread it several times, then finally typed in an unrecognised phone number and hit 'send'. He watched the screen until it flashed up 'Message sent', then closed his eyes again and dropped his head back against the leather.

He fell asleep with the words of his message scrolling through his mind: "How does an unwanted player switch teams? Be discreet."

Jimmy Coates slumped down outside the train toilet, exhausted. His senses allowed his pain to creep through him again. It didn't stop until he was aching and throbbing all over. The only consolation came when he realised that the next stop was London Bridge.

Only a couple of minutes later the train pulled in and

Jimmy staggered on to the platform. His mind was completely dazed. His agony seemed to intensify with every step, as if his body didn't want to let him relax. He couldn't help glancing over his shoulders, scanning the faces of everybody else who'd stepped off the train and everybody waiting along the platform. *Did they track me?* he asked himself.

He couldn't let his guard down. But as he limped through the station, he became fascinated to see the lives of Londoners going on around him as if nothing had happened that night. There were no NJ7 agents. Nobody shot at him. Nobody sprang an ambush.

Jimmy slowed to a complete stop in the centre of the main concourse. Nobody even seemed to notice him. If they'd ever known who he was, they didn't recognise him any more. They'd forgotten, distracted by the fresh news of an election, or by whatever was going on in their lives. His thoughts melted into a haze.

"Waiting for a train?" came a girl's voice from behind him. Jimmy snapped out of his daydream and spun round. It was his sister Georgie. Jimmy didn't even have time to draw breath before his sister wrapped him in a hug.

"How did you—?" Jimmy gasped, the breath being squeezed out of his lungs by Georgie's embrace. He was so shocked he couldn't even return the hug at first.

"Chris has his own surveillance on the whole station," Georgie answered. "You're going to love it. He's got a whole base set up in the vaults under the bridges. Come on – we've been waiting for you." She let Jimmy go and marched away towards one of the platforms. Jimmy followed, hardly able to believe this was real.

"He's here," Georgie said softly into a mobile phone. She snapped it shut straight away and slipped it back into her pocket. Jimmy suddenly remembered his own phone. He patted his pockets, but realised he must have dropped it back at the hospital when Mitchell had first attacked him.

"Georgie," he said. "My phone... Mum's, I mean..."

"Forget about that," Georgie told him, grabbing his arm and pulling him along. "You wouldn't be able to use it anyway. We have to change phones every few hours. You'll get the hang of it. Chris has everything organised."

Jimmy was still in shock, but finally he felt a smile forcing its way on to his lips. "There's going to be—"

"I know," Georgie interrupted. "An election. Chris is totally psyched about it. Now get a move on. NJ7 will have themselves organised again in a few minutes. We don't want to get killed before we've won the election, do we?"

That's when Jimmy saw the others: Christopher Viggo, Saffron Walden, his mum and Felix all hurrying across the concourse. Before he knew it, Jimmy was swamped at the centre of all of them, and everybody was talking at once.

"Well done, Jimmy," said Viggo.

Saffron beamed a huge smile. Jimmy's mother said something, but it was so muffled by her hug that

Jimmy couldn't make it out. For a moment they looked just like any of the ordinary families or groups of friends that were reunited at the station every day. For a few seconds, Jimmy felt like a normal life was close enough to touch.

When they moved away, the smiles faded. Jimmy felt warm having friends walking on either side of him, but he knew that they were all thinking the same thing: the battle for control of the country was about to begin.

"You look totally mashed up," said Felix, landing a punch on Jimmy's shoulder.

Jimmy forced a smile. "I feel fine," he lied, slipping his blue-tinged fingers into his pockets.

How many Jimmy Coates books have you read?

1. Jimmy Coates: Killer
Jimmy Coates is a boy with a secret and even he doesn't know what it is. But it's a matter of life and death...

2. Jimmy Coates: Target
On the run, Jimmy's newfound talents are tested to their limits. But how can he survive when his enemy's greatest weapon is a boy just like him?

About the author

Joe Craig is a novelist, screenwriter, songwriter and performer. His award-winning thrillers have earned him a place alongside Anthony Horowitz, Charlie Higson and Robert Muchamore as "one of the best spy kids authors... outstanding at both writing and plotting." (The Times) The first Jimmy Coates book was published by HarperCollins in 2005. Since then the series has won over fans across the world and converted thousands of previously reluctant readers with an electric mix of action, suspense and thrilling twists.

Packed houses at festivals, bookshops, libraries and schools all over the world have experienced The Joe Craig Show. His tall tales, improvised stories, and surprising theories about writing have enthralled and entertained audiences every bit as much as his books.

He studied Philosophy at Cambridge University then became a songwriter. His first solo album ('The Songman & Me') was released in 2011. The success of his books led to a new career writing movies. Now he splits his writing time between novels and film projects.

When he's not writing, (or even when he is) he's visiting schools, eating sushi, playing the piano, watching a movie, reading, drawing, playing snooker or cricket, inventing a new snack, cooking, doing martial arts training or sleeping.

He lives in London with his wife (broadcaster & adventurer Mary-Ann Ochota), his dog (Harpo the labradonkey) and his dwarf crocodile (Professor Sven). You can get in touch with him through his website (www.joecraig.co.uk) or facebook (www.facebook.com/joecraiguk).